EXCITE ME

EMILIA ROSE

Copyright © 2022 by Emilia Rose

All rights reserved.

This book or parts thereof may not be reproduced in any form, stored in any retrieval system, or transmitted in any form by any means—electronic, mechanical, photocopy, recording, or otherwise—without prior written permission of the author, except as provided by United States of America copyright law. For permission requests, write to the author at "Attention: Permissions Coordinator" at the email address below.

Any references to historical events, real people, or real places are used fictitiously. Names, characters, and places are products of the author's imagination.

Cover by: Deranged Doctor Designs

Editor: Jovana Shirley, Unforeseen Editing, www.unforeseenediting.com

Proofreading: Heart Full of Reads, Kirsten Clower, Tina Franco

Emilia Rose

emiliarosewriting@gmail.com

To all the girls who wished their best friends' dads were hot enough to bang.

CHAPTER 1

MIA

"Your pussy's so fucking tight, baby," Mason mumbled into my ear. His forearms were posted on either side of my head, and he pulled me close to him as he pumped into me. Locks of his blond hair stuck to his sweaty forehead.

"Oh, Mason," I whispered, closing my eyes. I wrapped my thighs around his waist, pushed a hand between my legs, and rubbed small circles around my clit to try to get off.

But before I could even get myself close, Mason pinned my wrists above my head with one hand, refusing to let me touch myself when he could be the one to do it himself. He pushed his hand between my legs, his fingers hitting my dry clit and making my legs jerk up.

All I wanted to do was scream out in pain, but I didn't say anything to him about it because the last time I had … he refused to touch me like this for months. He'd told me that he knew exactly what he was doing and that me pointing this out to him was me *ridiculing* him.

I squeezed my eyes closed, trying to think of something that could make me the slightest bit wet as his cock slammed into my raw pussy over and over again. My mind wandered from the cute guy at Mickey's Coffee Shop to my own damn college professor, yet none of them made this any better.

My pussy was dry, stinging, and now chafed. And I just wanted this night to be over.

So, I said what I always did when I didn't want to have sex with Mason anymore. "Come inside of me, Mason." I dug my nails into his back, pretending like I was enjoying him and silently thanked Mom for taking me to get that IUD years ago. "Fill my tight little pussy with all of your cum."

Mason grabbed my waist, his thumbs digging harshly into my sides. I clenched on him—I *made* myself tighten on him—and sucked in a breath.

"Oh, just like that. Please, I need it," I begged.

After a couple moments, he tensed, his hips seizing, and groaned into my ear. I gripped on to his shoulders, feeling his thick cum pump inside of me.

I lay on the bed, stared up at the plain, boring ceiling, and felt Mason roll off of me and onto his side.

With one forearm over his face and the other limp by his side, he muttered, "Damn, baby."

"Wow," I said, lips set in a tense line. "That was amazing." My words sounded so lifeless because, well, they were.

Another night of sex with Mason, only to be disappointed. I didn't know why I continued to get my hopes up that one day, I wouldn't have to perform in bed. After five years with him, I had only come from him a handful of times and … I blew out a deep breath … I couldn't even remember when the last time had been.

Despite all the bad things about Mason in bed, there was a bright side to this mess. He'd be snoring in three … two …

His breathing evened out, and he let out a throaty snore. I sighed and pushed a hand under the sheets. If Mason couldn't get me off, I knew what could.

My body relaxed against the bed, and I did what I did every night. I closed my eyes and thought of the hottest man I knew.

My best friend's father.

It was wrong. It was so wrong, but, God, did it feel right. Thinking of him always felt right.

I refused to think about Michael Bryne while Mason was inside me, because I knew him—closely. But I didn't really know the guy from the coffee shop or my college professor. I didn't talk to them. It was pure fantasy. But I saw Mr. Bryne more than a couple times a week. I talked to him. We exchanged looks and touches—none of which were sexual—but still...

A couple weeks ago, Michael had been fixing up the yard, dressed in one of his gray V-necks, his sleeves tight against his biceps. I took a deep breath, my pussy pulsing. When he tugged his shirt over his head...

Pleasure rolled through me. It was ... it was enough to drive me wild.

All I wanted was for his face to be buried deep between my legs, his eyes gazing up at me, his hot mouth all over my pussy, eating me until I came more than once. I knew that he'd do it too. I knew that he'd finish me over and over again. That man wasn't a quitter. He'd fuck me until I couldn't walk, and ... I would let him, if I ever had the chance.

I thought about Mr. Bryne way too many times. It was embarrassing to think that my best friend's father could affect me more than my boyfriend ever had. And, hell, Mr. Bryne had never even touched me.

Two of my fingers slipped into my pussy, sliding in and out so easily. I pounded them deeper, imagining that it was Michael Bryne's big cock jamming into my tight hole, imagining him above me, imagining my fingers digging into his back, my pussy pulsing all around him.

My palm hit my clit with every thrust, making the tension build higher and higher in my core. I arched my back, pinched my nipple between two fingers, and bit my lip, so I wouldn't scream his name.

Wave after wave of ecstasy pumped through me, and my whole body tingled. Another earth-shattering orgasm, lying in Mason's bed, fantasizing about an older man. I pulled my fingers out of my pussy, wiped them across my thigh, and turned onto my side to look at my very *lovely* boyfriend.

Mason was turned away from me, and I could only imagine drool dripping from his lips like it usually did. Even in his sleep, his muscles were tense. I frowned, guilt washing over me. Part of me wished Mason had given me the orgasm, so I wouldn't feel this bad about coming to a fantasy about my friend's father.

But what was even worse was that part of me didn't care at all. Every night he didn't try to make me come, I cared less and less about him. I even toyed with the idea of breaking up with him, but—I shook my head and turned to my side—I couldn't.

Mason turned toward me, wrapped an arm around my waist, and placed his nose against my neck, snoring into my ear. I closed my eyes. I couldn't break up with him. We'd been together for five years. So many memories. So many good times. So much I had to make up for.

My phone buzzed on the dresser, and I hopped up to see a *good night* text from Mom. I smiled at the little <3 instead of a heart emoji and promised her that I'd come see her at the hospital early Monday morning. She quickly texted me back.

Mom: Hope you and Mason are good. xx You two seemed off today.

I sighed and put my phone back down, climbing back into our bed. We had been *off* for the past two years, but I never told Mom that, not when she was in that state. I didn't tell her that he had refused to let me visit her unless he was with me either. I didn't tell her that Mason held her hospital bills that he paid for with his parents' money over my head. I didn't tell her any of it.

To her, Mason and I were perfect. And that's how it'd stay for the rest of my life.

At least I could relax for the next couple of days at Melissa's for our girls' weekend. There would be booze, boyfriend-free conversation, a pool to go skinny-dipping in at four in the morning, and of course—the only reason I was really going—Mr. Bryne.

CHAPTER 2

MIA

I bounced up and down on my toes, pulling Mason up the white-paved sidewalk toward Melissa's house. The house was bigger than the average home—two floors, about five thousand square feet, surrounded by acres of woods.

"You're really excited," Mason said, a tinge of jealousy in his voice. The wind blew softly, his golden locks falling onto his forehead. "Why don't you ever get this excited for me?"

After plastering a fake smile on my face, I looked over at him. "I always get this excited for you," I said, tucking some brown hair behind my ear.

He grimaced and even rolled his eyes.

"And besides, I haven't hung out with Melissa and Serena in so long. I've been working and visiting Mom. It's about time I got to spend a couple nights gossiping about you." I playfully poked his stomach, trying to get him to smile.

"Talk about me or all the guys in my frat you want to fuck?"

I stopped before we walked into the house. "What're you talking about?" I asked, brows drawn together.

He stared at me, nostrils flared. *What is his problem?*

He shook his head and seized the door handle. "Forget it."

I pulled his hand away and stared at him. "Forget what? What did I do?" I asked, reluctantly leaving out the *this time* part that I desperately wanted to add.

His jaw twitched. "You don't remember?" he asked, glaring down at me. "You fucking mumble their names in your sleep. Every night, I wake up to you moaning about someone else."

Mumble people's names in my sleep? I'd barely slept last night.

After narrowing my eyes at him, I crossed my arms over my chest. "Whose name did I say?" I asked, testing him.

Mason was a deep sleeper. If he didn't wake up when I turned my vibrator on full blast, he wouldn't wake up from me mumbling names in my sleep.

"Victor."

I raised my brows. "Victor? As in Melissa's boyfriend?"

That man was a total man-whore who only got girls because he had money. If that boy were poor, he'd have to beg for a woman's attention. A disrespectful sleazeball. Not my type.

"I wasn't dreaming of him last night," I said, placing my hand on my hip. "Why would you even think that, Mason? He's your best friend and my best friend's boyfriend."

He shook his head again, one of his many annoyed expressions crossing his face. "Forget it," he said. Then, he walked into the house, not bothering to hold the door open for me, leaving me behind.

I stared at the glass door, lips pinched into a tight line, foot tapping against the concrete sidewalk. *This fucking man.* I had done nothing. Absolutely nothing. And he thought he could—

"The door isn't going to open itself," someone said from behind me.

I stood up straighter, my cheeks tinting red, and turned on my heel to meet the piercing eyes of the one and only Mr. Bryne.

He twirled his car keys around his index finger and raised his brows at me as he walked up the sidewalk to the front door. Dressed in a fitted dress shirt, he had his suit jacket slung over his shoulder and his briefcase hanging off the other.

My cheeks warmed even more as I watched his biceps flex through the thin material. I smiled awkwardly at him, all my hazy fantasies dancing through my mind.

God, Mia, keep it together. Your boyfriend is just inside the house. Don't want him thinking you have a crush on Melissa's father now.

"Good evening, Mia," Mr. Bryne said, my name rolling off his full lips, like it had a million times since high school. He pulled the door open, gesturing for me to enter.

I grasped the handle, my fingers sweeping against his long ones. "Hi, Mr. Bryne." My fingers tingled at the contact, and I gulped.

It felt like years since I had seen him, but it had only been a few weeks. In high school, I'd see him every day, but now that we were in college, I only saw him when Melissa wanted to use his pool for a few days. So, I hopped on any chance I had to come over.

We stepped into the foyer.

"You're staying over this weekend?" he asked, lips parted as he stared down at me.

I clenched my pussy, imagining those full lips trailing down my neck, his fingers slipping into my underwear, his cock pressing against my entrance.

"Yep," I said, hoisting my backpack up my shoulder.

He smirked, his eyes growing wide and ... playful. "Well, I hope you girls have fun."

His gaze flickered down my body for a mere moment, and my cheeks flushed.

Stop it, Mia. He's probably just ... looking at the carpet.

He leaned toward me. "If you need me for *anything*, Mia, you know where to find me."

Then, he hiked the strap of his briefcase higher up his shoulder and walked up the stairs, his hand briefly brushing against mine as he passed.

His suit pants were tight against his ass—

"Mia!" Melissa called from downstairs.

I took a deep breath, pushing away my dirty thoughts, and walked downstairs, where Melissa was talking to Victor, Damien, and Mason on the couch.

When she saw me, she hopped up from her seat and grabbed my hand. "I'm so excited for this weekend! We can finally relax."

Serena pulled a couple bottles of tequila off Mr. Bryne's downstairs bar and walked to the couch, sitting next to Damien. "You guys staying for a drink?"

Victor looked at his phone. "Party doesn't start for a few hours. Pregame?"

Victor, Damien, and Mason were all part of the same college frat, Sigma Alpha Elision—or whatever the hell it was called. They threw ridiculously huge parties every weekend, where everyone either got smashed, got fucked, ended up in the hospital, or a bit of all three. I had been to one too many and was getting tired of it.

The guys stayed for an hour, finishing a whole bottle of tequila by themselves. I watched Mason drink one drink after another and thanked the gods above that I wouldn't have to deal with his ass after the party tonight.

I sipped on my glass, the alcohol making me woozy. Mr. Bryne walked downstairs, still in his damn suit. He grabbed a glass, sighed through his nose, his back muscles relaxing, and poured himself a drink.

Damien stood up from the couch, placing the bottle on a side table and checking his phone. "You guys ready to get fucked up?"

I rolled my eyes, taking a deep breath through my nose, and

watched Damien kiss Serena good-bye and Victor hug Melissa. Mason nodded at me like I was one of his friends and squeezed my shoulder.

No kiss on the lips. Just a measly shoulder squeeze and a half-hearted good-bye. I stared at his departing frame, a frown stretching across my face. The front door shut behind the guys, and Melissa laughed.

"They're going to get plastered tonight." She grabbed her glass and a bottle of wine, nodding toward the stairs to her bedroom. "Come on. Let's go."

Serena popped up after her, following her toward her bedroom. I sighed, feeling bad that Mason showed no ounce of affection toward me anymore, and stood up.

Mr. Bryne glanced over at me, his biceps flexing. I looked at him for a moment longer than I should've. He didn't break eye contact with me, just turned around and leaned against the bar.

Grabbing my drink from the table, I begged myself to look at his face and his face only. *Nowhere else, Mia.* Not at those lips curled into a smirk. Not at his taut muscles. Not at the bulge in his pants.

I sipped my glass and stared over at him. His deep, gray eyes were playful again.

"Is there something wrong, Mia?" he asked, voice low.

I parted my lips, unable to form any coherent words.

Mason. Think about Mason.

But all I could think about was Mr. Bryne placing me on the bar counter and fucking me senseless. His full lips all over my body. His teeth biting gently into my neck. His fingers—those long fingers—rubbing my clit the way I did every night.

"Mia!" Melissa shouted from the bedroom. "Are you coming?"

I blinked a few times and stepped to the side, trying to think clearly. Then, without another word, I walked past him.

"It's not my place to say anything," Mr. Bryne said before I walked up the stairs.

I stopped and looked back.

He paused for a moment and stared back at me. "Your boyfriend."

"What about Mason?"

His tongue glided against his teeth, his jaw tight. "He should treat you better."

After staring at him for a few moments more, I nodded and walked up the stairs, taking deep breaths to calm myself down. "He should," I whispered to myself.

CHAPTER 3

MIA

Blonde hair falling into her face, Melissa rolled onto her stomach and typed about a million miles an hour on her phone with her lips set in a small smile. It was almost three in the morning. Serena was passed out on the couch in Melissa's room, and I was trying to sleep.

Her phone's brightness must've been turned all the way up because I could see it through my damn closed eyes. I squinted one eye open so I didn't go blind, and stared at the door. Maybe if I got something to drink or went to the bathroom or told her I couldn't sleep, she'd get the hint and turn it off.

The hallway light suddenly turned on, and I opened my eyes fully, listening to Mr. Bryne's footsteps out in the hallway.

Control yourself, Mia. You don't have to go out there. Tell Melissa that you're tired and hope that she'll turn off her phone.

"Jeez, Victor is still awake?" I asked.

Melissa's blue eyes widened, and she dimmed her phone screen. "Sorry. Yeah, that boy can drink until sunrise."

I gave her a half-hearted smile and turned onto my side, gazing at my phone that had zero—and I mean, zero—messages from Mason. I'd texted him earlier—quite a few times—only for him to ignore every single one of them. After sighing, I gazed back out at the light blaring under the door from the hallway.

Relax, Mia.

Melissa continued typing away, her blue manicured nails clacking against the screen.

"I'm going to the bathroom," I said, scrambling out of bed and sneaking into the hallway. I closed the door and wandered down the hallway, past the bathroom and over to the living room sliding glass door.

I walked out onto the deck and sat on one of the plush navy-colored patio seats. A breeze blew through the woods, giving me goose bumps on my exposed legs. I rested on the seat and looked down by the pool, where Mr. Bryne was sitting by the fireplace. His back was turned toward me, his muscles rippling against his white T-shirt.

"God," I whispered, taking a deep breath.

What am I even doing out here? It was late.

So damn late.

With his phone to his ear, I listened to him sigh. My heart pounded against my chest, all those dirty little fantasies coming to my mind. I closed my eyes.

Control, Mia.

For the first time tonight, I listened to him speak to the person on the other end, his voice deep and gruff. I squeezed my knees together and rubbed my palm against my thigh.

Don't think about it.

I ground my thighs together, hoping for some kind of friction. He paused for a few moments, said a couple more words, then stood up.

"Fuck," I whispered under my breath, bucking my hips against the patio chair. "Fuck me."

He walked around the pool, the moonlight bouncing off his tan skin. I stared down at him, slipping a hand between my legs. This was the one and only time I'd touch myself at his house. It wouldn't happen again. I was just really, really stressed and horny and ... God, he looked so damn good in those sweatpants.

I rubbed myself through my shorts. I'd only do it for a few moments. Not any longer. *Not*—my fingers massaged my clit —*fucking*—a rush of pleasure shot through me—*longer* ...

I closed my eyes, took a deep breath, and rubbed my fingers even faster against my pussy. The force was rising inside of me, and all I could imagine were his rough hands all over my body, his soft lips brushing against mine as he told me all the things he had been wanting to do to me. I stifled a moan, so close to coming.

When I reopened my eyes to stare at him, knowing it would tip me over the edge, he had turned in my direction, but he hadn't looked up. At least, I hoped he hadn't.

Though I wanted to stop myself so he couldn't have a chance to catch me, I continued. My pussy was pulsing, aching for a sweet release because I hadn't felt this good in so long. But when Mr. Bryne glanced up at the deck, I froze. Quickly, he glanced back down at the pool, watching the moonlight glimmer off of it, and I rubbed my pussy faster, hoping I could come in the .02 seconds when he looked away. Maybe he hadn't seen me.

But ... he clicked the phone off and looked back up. "Mia," he said, staring up at the deck. "What're you doing up? It's almost three in the morning."

I leaned forward, trying not to make it obvious that I was indeed touching myself to him out here. "I, um ..." I stood up, my nipples pressing against my crop top. I leaned over the edge of the deck, resting my forearms on the ledge. A wind blew again, my loose orange crop top blowing with it. "I couldn't sleep."

He paused for a moment, his jaw clenching. He stood directly below, looking up at me. And there wasn't a doubt in my mind that he could see right up my shirt. My pussy tightened even more at the thought of Mr. Bryne seeing me naked and actually enjoying the view.

"Neither could you, huh?" I asked, trying to ease the tension.

He paused for a moment.

"Come down here," he said.

"Me?" I asked stupidly, my cheeks flaming. "I don't know—Melissa will probably come looking for me."

"Come down here," he said again without giving me room to argue.

I hurried back inside, leaving the deck sliding door ajar, and walked down the stairs to the pool. Mr. Bryne met me at the bottom and handed me a glass of wine. I grabbed it from him, touching his fingers, and followed him to the patio. The mere feeling of his fingers on mine drove me wild, and I sat across from him.

My eyes landed on the pool as I sipped my wine and tried to stop my cheeks from flushing. When I glanced over at him, his eyes flickered to my tits. His jaw tightened, and he looked away, taking a deep breath.

Is Mr. Bryne ... checking me out?

I shifted in my seat, trying to suppress the ache between my legs, but with every moment, that ache was intensifying. Maybe he was just wondering why I wasn't wearing a bra or how I must be so damn cold out here.

His phone buzzed on the chair next to him. He glanced down at it and sipped his wine, sighing through his nose.

"You should get that," I said quietly.

He turned his phone over and shut it off. "I can't talk to her again."

"Her?" I asked.

"Melissa's mother," he said, rubbing his forehead.

Melissa spent some time at her mother's house mainly when we were in high school, but she never brought me, and she never told me what had happened between her parents years ago. All I knew was that one night, Mr. Bryne and Melissa's mother had gotten into a huge fight, and Melissa had come over to my house, crying.

I frowned and sipped my wine, squeezing my knees together. His stare dropped to my legs, and my breath caught in the back of my throat. I took another gulp of my wine, bucking my hips. It happened almost instinctively, and my pussy pulsed.

Mr. Bryne pressed his lips together, sipped his drink, and stared at the ground near my legs. I moved my ass against the chair again, grinding it back and forth, not able to stop myself. It was three in the morning, this wine was strong as hell, and I was horny.

"Mia," he said quietly.

"Yes, Mr. Bryne?" I said, clutching the side of the chair.

His gaze drifted to my tits again and to the way my nipples stiffened against the material. He rubbed his leg with his hand. "You should probably go to bed," he said quietly.

I stared at him with wide eyes. My lips parted, and then I pursed them back together. "But ..."

"But?" he asked, struggling to keep eye contact with me.

"But I'm not tired," I said before I could stop myself.

His jaw twitched, his eyes hardening. The way he was trying not to stare only made me more excited. I couldn't resist moving my ass against the seat.

"Well ..." He gulped, placed his glass on the table, and stood. "I'm going to head up." He walked over to me, squeezed my shoulder from behind—his touch inviting—then said, "Don't worry about staying quiet out here."

I tensed and stared down at my thighs. *What does he mean by that? Wh—*

"Good night, Mia." He opened the sliding glass door, then disappeared behind it.

My eyes stayed glued to my thighs, brows drawn together.

When I knew he was out of sight, I pushed my hand down my shorts and rubbed my aching clit.

The tension had built so high in my core that I didn't need much to get me going. *What ... does Mr. Bryne ...*

Fuck, I had been so close to letting him watch me touch myself, so close to letting *him* touch *me*.

He had been tempted. He was staring. He wanted it. And all I'd wanted was for him to come over.

My pussy clenched.

For him to strip off his pants.

For him to fuck me senseless.

I arched my back lightly, my legs starting to tremble.

I bit my lip, trying to be as quiet as I could. I slipped my hand under my shirt and pinched one of my nipples, and a loud moan escaped my lips before I could stop it. I slapped a hand over my mouth, threw my head back, and rode out my orgasm.

And when I finally came down from it, I listened to the sliding glass door on the deck close and watched Mr. Bryne walk deeper into the dark house.

CHAPTER 4

MIA

I yawned and turned onto my side. The sunlight flooded in through the window. I blinked my eyes open, smelling the bitter scent of coffee drifting into the room. Melissa and Serena were gone, the bedroom door ajar. I pushed the blankets off of me and padded out into the hallway, following the sweet scent of breakfast.

"It's about time," Melissa said from the kitchen table.

She and Serena were chatting over a box of doughnuts. Mr. Bryne was leaning against the counter with a coffee mug in his hand and a pair of tight gray sweatpants around his hips.

He glanced over at me, smirking. I gulped and avoided eye contact with him, my heart racing in my chest. Something about that damn stare of his made me think that he really had watched me from the deck last night and that he *enjoyed* it.

I hurried around the granite kitchen table and sat in a chair, snatching a doughnut. I yawned again, tiredness washing over me. "What time is it?"

"Almost eleven." Melissa broke a jelly doughnut over a napkin and stuffed it into her mouth. "You were up late."

I snuck a glance at Mr. Bryne, who was licking cream from his Boston cream doughnut off his lips.

He raised a brow at me. "I heard you out by the pool, Mia. What were you up to?"

I narrowed my eyes at him for a moment, watching his brow arch ever so slightly. If he'd heard me, then he knew what had happened. I squeezed my legs together, feeling heat pool between them.

"Were you texting Mason?" Serena asked, gazing down at her phone, then staring up at me and waiting for my answer.

"Um … yeah." I bit into my doughnut. "He wanted to talk last night."

"Did you two get into a fight?" Mr. Bryne asked, taking another sip of his coffee. "You were being awfully loud."

My heart raced. *Is Mr. Bryne flirting with me ... right in front of his daughter?*

I tightened at the thought. The nerve this man had excited me more than it should have. He didn't care who saw or who heard.

"I … we …" I didn't know how to respond with Melissa and Serena sitting right at the table with me. And, hell, I didn't know what kind of response he expected from me. *Does he want me to flirt back?*

I glanced at Serena and Melissa, who were both too occupied with their phones, especially Melissa. "Yes, we did." Lie. I sat up in my seat, pressed my breasts against the table, and looked over at him. "Was I too loud for you, Mr. Bryne?"

He smirked, his eyes growing wide and playful again. For a moment, his gaze dropped to my nipples taut against the table, and then he looked back up at me. "No," he said, dropping his hand so his coffee mug covered the bulge forming in his sweatpants. "I wanted you to be louder."

My pussy tensed, and I glanced at Serena and Melissa, who

seemed to be in their own little worlds. My cheeks flushed, my nipples aching. God, he really was flirting with me.

I leaned back in my seat, the pressure rising in my pussy. Like last night, I had the urge to rub one out ... but I couldn't do it now. Not here. Not when Melissa and Serena were sitting at the table with me.

All I wanted was for him to move that coffee mug, so I could see what I had been aching to see for a long time now. I furrowed my brows, watching him smirk at me and bring the coffee mug to his lips to sip.

I clenched even harder, my pussy pulsing. God, it was so fucking big. I wanted it inside of me, ramming into my tight little hole. Filling me all the way up. Stuffing me full. Making me come over and over again.

Control, Mia. Control yourself.

Melissa placed her phone facedown on the table and stuffed another piece of her doughnut into her mouth. "What do you guys want to do today?"

Your father.

She finished chewing. "I scheduled a matching mani-pedi for twelve, then the pool?"

Serena agreed, and I nodded along with her. Hell, I didn't care what we did as long as we came back here. I wanted Mr. Bryne, and I wanted him bad. I hadn't wanted anyone like I wanted him in a long time ... like since Mason and I had started dating.

Melissa hopped up from her seat. "I'm going to take a shower." She finished her coffee and put her mug into the dishwasher.

Serena sighed and stood, holding her phone to her ear. "Damien, what do you want? I said it was a girls' weekend." She walked right out of the room and left me to stew in front of Mr. Bryne.

After a couple moments, he placed his mug down on the counter and walked over to me. Every step he took, I moved my knees closer and closer together. His gray eyes were locked on to mine, his lips pulled into a smirk.

My pussy was tightening when he reached me, my nipples tight against my top.

"Can I help you?" I asked, staring at my bare thighs.

He reached for my chin. "Look at me when you talk," he said.

I stared up at him, my heart pounding in my chest. With one hand gripping onto my chin, he reached his other hand lower, drawing his fingers up the inside of my thigh.

Almost instinctively, I parted my legs for him. I curled my feet around the legs of the chair and hoped that he would feel how wet I was for him. It was beyond wrong. I knew that, but I did it anyway.

Inch by inch, his fingers moved higher up my thigh, and then they hovered right over my wetness. I gulped, my pussy aching. I parted my lips and tried to get out the word *please*, but nothing would come out. I could feel the heat radiating from his fingers.

Please. Please. Please. It was one simple word.

Then, almost as if he wanted to hold himself back, he released my chin and pulled his fingers away from my pussy. I gulped, all those dirty little fantasies escaping me.

"Did you sleep well last night, Mia?"

I leaned forward a couple inches, letting my breasts graze against his bulge. "Is that really what you wanted to ask?"

He chuckled, regaining his composure. "No." He brushed his fingertips against my inner thigh again, rubbing them back and forth in soothing circles, and then ... he shoved them against my shorts. "I wanted to ask how wet you were for me." Pushing my shorts to the side, he slipped his fingers under them and rubbed my clit through my underwear. "But I thought it was inappropriate."

My eyes widened, and I looked up. The tension rose in my core. I clutched the sides of the seat, fingers digging into the wood. *Oh God. Oh God. Oh God. Oh God.* He started to rub my pussy, his fingers moving fast against the fabric.

"So, I thought I'd see for myself."

His gaze drifted from my pussy to my tits to my eyes, as he rubbed me faster. This was wrong. This was so wrong. I tightened, wishing he'd slip a finger under my panties and push it right inside of me.

"Is this what you did last night?" he asked, fingers moving faster. "Touched your wet little pussy out by the pool when I left?"

I gulped and licked my lips, grazing two fingers against my nipples. "You watched me, didn't you?" I asked.

He chuckled, smiling. "It's not like you didn't want me to."

He drew a finger around my nipple, and then he clasped it between his fingers and tugged on it, shaking my breast up and down. Pleasure rushed through me, and he leaned down, his lips against my ear.

"I bet you were thinking about me." He continued to rub my pussy, making the tension build inside me. "I bet all you could think about was my cock thrusting inside of you instead of your fingers."

My eyes dropped to the bulge in his pants, and I furrowed my brows. It was so fucking big. All I wanted was to—

"Go ahead, Mia." He chuckled deeply into my ear. "Touch it."

The force drove me higher and higher. I reached out, touching the front of his pants, and as soon as I did ... I came.

"Mia!" Melissa yelled.

I sighed through my nose, trying to keep quiet and to stop my legs from shaking.

"I'm coming, Melissa." And I really was.

CHAPTER 5

MIA

We got our nails painted, drove two hours both ways to get this dairy-free ice cream that Melissa had been dying for, stopped at a farm on our way home so Serena could take pictures with five little ducklings, and then almost got into a car accident because Melissa's phone was buzzing in her lap while she was driving.

It was almost two in the morning when we got home, and both Serena and Melissa were hyped up tonight.

Now, they were lying on the bed, kicking their legs back and forth and gossiping. I lay on the couch and stared up at the ceiling, starting to think that maybe a weekend was too long.

"Victor is sooo good! He literally makes me come every time," Melissa said, fanning herself.

I closed my eyes and took a deep breath.

"Damien is the same way!" Serena said. "He does this thing with his tongue, and, oh my God, I can't handle it!"

I had been listening to them talk nonstop about their

boyfriends for the past ten hours. Which one was better in bed. Which one had a bigger dick. Which one ate pussy better. It was getting damn annoying because Mason, my *lovely* boyfriend, was shit.

"Must be nice," I said, chiming in for the first time tonight.

"Oh, come on," Melissa said, sitting up and throwing a pillow at me. "Mason can't be that bad."

I raised an eyebrow at her. "We've been together for five years, and he's made me come, like, five times," I said, annoyance in my voice. It wasn't that I cared all about the sex … but I just wanted some effort.

"Are you serious?" Serena asked in disbelief. "I thought you said he always ate you out."

"He does, but that doesn't mean he's good at it." I rubbed a hand over my face. "I have to fake an orgasm just to get him to stop because it's so bad."

Mason wasn't completely terrible. Sometimes, he would hit a spot on my clit, and I'd moan.

"You could always break up with him and find yourself a new man who'd do you right. What about Victor's older brother?" Melissa winked at me. "He's hot." She fanned herself. "I've thought about him way too many times."

I shook my head in her direction. I didn't need her trying to set me up with anyone. I needed Mason. He had been with me through all the heartbreak, through Mom's accident, when Dad had left. All of it.

Someone knocked on Melissa's door.

"Yeah?"

The door opened, and Mr. Bryne stuck his head into the room, giving her a pointed look. "It's almost three in the morning."

He glanced at me, and I tore my attention away from him and stared at the ceiling.

Don't think about earlier, Mia. Don't get yourself into more trouble. You have Mason.

What had happened earlier couldn't happen again. Ever again.

"Sorry, Dad. We'll be quiet," Melissa said.

After he left the room, they turned back to me.

"So, should I call Victor's brother and talk to him for you? Or do you want me to give you his number and you can do it yourself?"

I bit my lip, making it seem like I was contemplating. "I'll pass for now, but I'll keep that in mind," I said. I wasn't going to keep that in mind, but I knew if I hadn't told her that, she'd have kept bothering me about it.

"Oh, okay," she said.

They turned back to each other and started back up with the constant *my boyfriend is better; no, mine; no, mine* battle they were having.

"I'm going to go get something to drink. Do you want me to get you anything?" I asked.

They shook their heads at me and continued to talk about their boyfriends.

"Mine's better."

"No, mine's better."

"Well, mine does—"

I walked out of Melissa's room and down the hall toward the kitchen. Mr. Bryne was sitting at the table, holding a drink in his hand. I innocently smiled at him and walked over to the cupboard.

I'd said I wasn't going to do anything with him tonight, and I wasn't going to. I just needed some water. That was all.

I stood on my toes to reach for a glass on the top shelf. My shorts rode up my legs as I stretched out. My fingers barely grazed against it. I sighed and reached for it again.

Mr. Bryne placed his hand on my lower back, and I jumped.

"I'll get it for you," he said.

Goose bumps darted across my skin at his touch as I remembered the way he'd touched me earlier. His hardness grazed up against my backside as he reached for the cup.

I closed my eyes and clenched. He pushed himself against me and finally grabbed the cup. When he placed it on the counter in front of me, he brushed his fingers against mine.

"Thanks," I breathed out.

"Not a problem," he said.

I could feel his lips on my ear, his cock slowly sliding itself into my tight pussy. He walked back over to his seat, and I took a deep breath, hoping to regain control of myself. I walked to the sink, swaying my hips just enough to keep his attention, and filled the glass.

He sighed. "Mia, we have to stop playing this game."

I shut off the tap and looked at him. "What are you talking about?"

"You know what I'm talking about," he said.

When I pursed my lips in his direction, he closed his eyes and placed his hand under the table.

I shook my head and smirked. "No, I don't actually."

He swore under his breath as his eyes traveled down my body, lingering on my curves. His gaze met mine once more, and then he walked over to me. "Let me show you then."

He took the glass out of my hand and placed it on the counter next to us. My heart raced as he roughly pushed me up against the counter and lifted me, so I sat on it. He pushed himself between my legs and rubbed his dick against my throbbing core.

I placed a hand on his chest, feeling the muscle underneath his shirt, and tightened. "Mr. Bryne, I have a boyfriend." But that hadn't stopped me before … and as bad as it was, it wasn't going to stop me again.

He grabbed the glass of water I had poured, his finger tracing the edge of it. "A boyfriend who can't make you come," he said.

My cheeks warmed. He must've heard the conversation we were having earlier.

He pushed his hips closer to mine. "A boyfriend who doesn't excite you anymore." He took one of his hands off of the glass and rubbed it against my shorts like he had this morning. "I bet your boyfriend doesn't make you this wet anymore," he murmured against my ear.

I squeezed my legs as his fingers moved against my clit.

"You need a man, Mia, not a boy."

My nipples stiffened underneath my shirt as the force built in my pussy. I reached up and pinched them lightly, letting myself enjoy the moment. He kissed below my jaw, and I whimpered.

"I can excite you, Mia," he breathed, placing another kiss on my neck, his fingers toying with my pussy.

"Excite me then, Mr. Bryne."

"Whatever you say." He smirked, and then he brought the glass of water to his lips and sipped it.

I raised an eyebrow at him as he watched me. He licked his lips and moved the glass to my lips, wanting me to take one as well.

This wasn't what I had expected when he said he was going to excite me. I furrowed my brows. His smirk widened as he pushed the glass closer to my lips. I guessed I would go along with it.

I parted my lips and moved them closer to the cup. He tilted the glass, letting the water spill out of it. He purposely missed my mouth, and the coldness of the water ran down the front of my thin white tank top, making it see-through.

"Oops," he said, gazing down at my chest with hungry gray eyes. "Sorry."

The shirt was plastered up against my nipples. His fingers crawled up my body, and he took my nipples gently between his fingers and pulled on them.

I gripped the edge of the counter and threw my head back as heat rushed to my core.

"I've been waiting to see these for so long," he murmured. He dipped his head and grazed his teeth against my wet shirt while he snaked his hands under it to grope my breasts.

He pressed his lips to mine. I dug my fingers into his shoulders and pulled him closer to me, loving the feeling of his cock against my shorts.

"I need you," I said against him. I didn't want to fucking wait anymore. I didn't want to be disappointed night after night after night. I gripped his thick hair in my hand and pulled back enough to look him in the eyes. "Fuck me, please."

He undid the button on his pants, unzipped them, and pulled them down just enough to take out his dick. I pushed down my shorts and underwear. He positioned himself at my entrance, rubbed his cock against my wet pussy, and groaned.

And within a moment, he plunged into me. My pussy wrapped around his cock, like it had never felt anything so big inside of me, and clenched on him each time he pumped into me.

His eyes traveled from my swollen clit to my wet T-shirt, and he watched my tits bounce as he fucked me.

"Harder," I begged.

He wrapped his arms around my knees as he pounded inside of me.

I bit my lip to muffle my moans. My legs began trembling. He tugged on both of my nipples harshly, and my back arched. I threw my head back and moaned.

"Mia! How long does it take you to get a glass of water?" Melissa yelled from her room.

My eyes widened, and I tightened around Mr. Bryne's shaft.

He covered my mouth with his hand as he continued to thrust into me. Tension was building inside me again. A few moments later, I heard footsteps down the hall.

I tried to stop Mr. Bryne, but he stayed inside of me. He wrapped my legs around his waist as he picked me up off of the counter, bringing us to the next room—the living room. There wasn't a door; only a doorway. He kept the light off and gently placed me down behind the couch. Even though the room was dark, I could still see the smirk on his face.

He knelt, lifted my legs in the air, and placed them on his shoulders.

"What are you doing?" I whisper-yelled at him.

"Giving you a damn good time," he said.

He shoved himself into me more forcefully than before, and I tried to hold back my moans.

"Mia! Where are you?" Melissa's footsteps padded around the kitchen.

Mr. Bryne held his hand to my mouth as he fucked me. I moaned into it and gripped the rug underneath me. His fingers teased my nipple through my wet shirt, and I tightened around him.

"Mia?" Melissa called out through the doorway to the living room.

Fuck, she was going to find us. Mr. Bryne drove deeper inside of me, his hand trailing down my body to my swollen clit. His fingers massaged circles around it. I bit down on my lip, desperately trying to keep quiet.

"Mia?" she said again.

My legs shook as the tension between them became unbearable. She walked out of the kitchen, and I threw my head back and moaned into Mr. Bryne's hand.

My lips parted. *Oh my God.* Gush after gush of pleasure pumped through me. He smirked down at me and pulled himself out.

When I finally came down from my orgasm, he lay down next to me, pulled me on top of him—placing my pussy near his face—wrapped his hand in my hair, and forced my head onto his cock.

I swirled my tongue around his cock, tasting my juices, and slowly took him all the way down my throat. He shoved my head down further for me to take more of his huge dick. I bobbed my head up and down on his length, and he began pumping his cock into my mouth.

"Mia!" Serena yelled.

"Mia! Where'd you go?" Melissa called.

I stopped sucking.

"Don't fucking stop," Mr. Bryne mumbled against my pussy. He flicked my clit with his tongue and drove me back down onto him. "I wanna see your tits bounce as you suck my cock."

He bobbed my head up and down on his cock, harder than before.

Their footsteps approached the kitchen.

I gagged on him as he hit the back of my throat. He grazed his hand against one of my breasts, took my nipple between his fingers, and twisted. *Holy—*

"Mia!" Serena yelled.

I sucked on his cock as he continued pleasuring my clit and nipple. His tongue made quicker circles on my clit, and I furrowed my brows, unsure if I would be able to hold myself together.

"Do you think she left?" Melissa asked from the kitchen.

"Why would she leave without telling us?" Serena answered.

They quieted down, and then their footsteps approached the living room.

"Did you check in here?" Serena asked.

Nerves zipped through me, but I continued sucking on Mr. Bryne's cock like he wanted me to. I shoved him deep down my throat and gagged quietly on it. His hand pushed my head down further on him and made me stay there.

I tried to breathe out of my nose and gagged once more. I needed to breathe.

The light turned on, and I froze. Fear and excitement stirred within me at the thought of getting caught. As long as I kept quiet, we wouldn't be.

"I already checked in there," Melissa said.

Mr. Bryne's tongue massaged my clit faster as his fingers pushed deep inside of me. The sound of my wet pussy being thrust into over and over overwhelmed me. There was no doubt that they could hear it.

He continued shoving his fingers inside of me, and his tongue lightly flicked the top of my clit. I released myself onto him, pushing him deeper down my throat and hoping that his cock would muffle my moans.

"Did you hear that?" Serena asked.

"Hear what?" Melissa said as she walked back into the kitchen.

It was quiet for a moment, and I pressed my lips firmer to his cock, so I wouldn't make a noise. The rapture continued to course out of me.

His warm cum hit the back of my throat and slid down it. I almost gagged. He chuckled quietly against my pussy, the sound vibrating my sensitive skin.

She turned off the light. "Nothing. I must be hearing things."

Their footsteps retreated out of the kitchen, and I gasped for air and moaned at the same time. I slid off of him and onto the ground. He pulled me closer to him and smirked.

"You ready for more?" he asked.

"How can you ask that?! We almost got caught—twice—by your daughter, who is my best friend!"

"Only a couple more times, and I will have made you come the same number of times in one night as your boyfriend has in five years."

I closed my eyes, then sighed and climbed back on top of him. "Excite me, Mr. Bryne."

CHAPTER 6

MIA

I straddled Mr. Bryne's waist, placed my hands on his chest, and closed my eyes, letting him thrust into me over and over. My shirt clung to my tits as they bounced with every pump. His gaze flickered from my eyes to my lips to my breasts, and he lifted his head. Through my wet shirt, he latched his teeth onto my nipple and sucked. His tongue moved around it in circles, flicking the sensitive bud every so often.

The pressure rose in my core, and I dug my fingernails into his chest, a wave of pleasure shooting through me. "Harder, Mr. Bryne ... please."

He drove up into me and bit down on my nipple gently. But it was enough for me to tip over the edge. My pussy pulsed over and over on his cock, the ecstacy getting me high.

"Did you just come?" he asked, brows arched, teeth biting down softly onto my nipple again.

I whimpered and collapsed onto him until my breasts were flush against his chest.

God, I didn't know what it was about this man ... but this was more than I'd ever fantasized.

He rolled me onto my side, turned me over so my back was against his chest, and pulled one of my legs high up in the air, shoving his cock back into me again. It slid in with ease, his size creating more tension. He slipped his arm around my waist and rubbed my clit as he rammed into me.

"Tell me, Mia ..." he said into my ear. "Tell me everything you think about when you touch your sensitive little pussy."

I pressed my lips together, bucking my hips back and forth and meeting his. I didn't want to admit it out loud. I didn't want to tell him that I had been thinking about fucking him for years now.

"Do you think about me?" he asked, steadying his thrusts. When I clenched on him, he chuckled. "You do." He paused for a moment, his fingers moving faster against my clit. "I bet you think about me when Mason fucks you."

My pussy tightened even harder.

"Mr. Bryne ..."

"I think about you," he said, and it was enough to tip me over the edge. "I've been thinking about what it would feel like to be inside of you for longer than I should admit."

Ecstasy exploded through me.

"I think about you," I said breathlessly. "Every night ... every fucking night." My legs and arms tingled. "Every night when Mason goes to bed, I rub my pussy and imagine you inside of me."

He plunged into me, lifting my leg and giving himself better access.

"I imagine you sucking on my tits, your hands roaming all over my body. I think about ... about ..."

"About what, Mia?"

"About you coming inside me."

Mr. Bryne tensed behind me, groaning loudly into my ear. He

pulled his cock out of me, pushed me onto my chest, and pressed his cock against my ass. When I felt his warm cum squirt out on me, I curled my toes. God, this couldn't be real.

After a few moments, his body relaxed behind me, but he didn't fall asleep, like Mason always did. Instead, he brushed his fingers against my hip bone in small, smoothing circles and breathed deeply into my ear.

Something about it was so calming even though it really shouldn't be.

He grasped my hip, fingers digging into it lightly, and hopped up, grabbing a paper towel from the kitchen and wiping his cum off my ass and then throwing it away.

When he came back into the room, swinging my shorts around in his hand, I stood up and pulled my underwear up my thighs.

"Well …" I started. The moonlight flooded in through the window, hitting his face almost perfectly. I could see almost every sharp feature of his face—from his jaw to his piercing gray eyes. I readjusted myself and looked at him. "Um … thank you?" Those were the only damn words that came out of my mouth. Because … well … what was I supposed to say to my best friend's father after he had given me the best sex of my entire life?

"You shouldn't have to thank a man for pleasing you," he said, handing me my shorts. Though I expected to see a lightness in his eyes, there was nothing but pure seriousness.

I peered at the ground, taking a deep breath, then looked back up at him. I didn't want to see Mason after that—my guilty conscience hadn't set in yet—but I couldn't go back into Melissa's room without an excuse, without her asking me a million and one questions about where I had been.

"Can you… uhm, bring me back to Mason's?" I asked nervously.

"So you can lie in his bed, feeling satisfied for once?" He laughed lifelessly. "No."

"I can't go back into Melissa's room," I said, voice hushed. "She's going to ask what I was doing and why I ignored her. What am I supposed to tell her? That I just slept with her father?"

He smirked at me, his eyes playful again. "You could."

"No." I sucked my lip between my teeth. "Please …"

"It's almost three in the morning," he said, crossing his arms over his chest. "You either go back into my daughter's room and act like I didn't just fuck your pussy raw or you come lie down in my room and I'll do it again."

I gulped. Again? He wanted to do it again? *I* wanted to do it again too … but I couldn't. I couldn't allow myself to do it again, no matter how much I wanted it.

"Good night," I said to him, hurrying toward Melissa's room before I changed my mind. I quietly opened the door, hoping that she wasn't awake and that she wouldn't wake up.

CHAPTER 7

MIA

"Mia," Melissa said from her bed, her voice sleepy.

I shut the door quietly behind me and clenched my jaw. *Damn it.*

"Mia!" Melissa whisper-yelled. The moonlight flooded in through the curtains, hitting her face. Serena was in the bed with her, eyes closed, lips parted. "Where were you?"

I padded into the room, my heart pounding against my chest. What the hell did I say to her? That every part of my body had been craving her father's touch since the moment I had laid eyes on him yesterday evening and that it had finally happened tonight? That Mr. Bryne had fucked me hard and fast and—

"Mia?" Melissa sat up. "Are you okay?"

"I, um … wasn't feeling too good." I climbed onto the couch and lay down on my side, facing away from the bed.

"What's wrong?"

"Nothing. I had a stomach ache." I tugged my knees to my chest and rolled my eyes. "I needed some fresh air."

"Are you okay?" she asked.

I took a deep breath, so I wouldn't flip out on her and closed my eyes. "Yes, Melissa."

The bed shifted, and she lay back down. I sank into the couch, feeling more satisfied than I ever had in my entire life. But then … then it really settled in. I'd had sex with Mr. Bryne. I'd had sex with my best friend's father. I had Mason.

My mind had been fogged with so much lust that I … I … cheated. My heart ached, and I held myself tighter, wishing that I could be in the arms of someone who would comfort me. But like it hadn't happened the other night with Mason, it wouldn't happen tonight with Mr. Bryne.

No matter how much I tried to think that I'd do things differently if I had the chance, I knew that I wouldn't. Mr. Bryne had actually wanted to please me tonight. He made sure I came over and over and over again, didn't stop until I lay on top of him, my chest heaving up and down, completely and utterly satisfied.

And that only made the guilt even more unbearable.

I had done the one thing that I'd sworn I'd never do. I had become like my father.

* * *

THE NEXT MORNING, I avoided Mr. Bryne by waking up super early and making an excuse that I felt sick, so sick that I had to go back home to Mason's immediately. It wasn't that I didn't want to see Mr. Bryne; it was that I knew if I did see him … I'd feel even guiltier.

So, I had snuck back into the apartment without Mason waking up, then when he finally had, he drove us to Oranegate Assisted Living to see Mom. I hopped out of Mason's Benz and grabbed his hand, walking toward the entrance. While there were a lot of shitty things about Mason, this was his most redeeming quality. He cared enough for Mom that he paid my mother's way here with his parents' money.

The automatic sliding doors opened, and Mason led the way into the building. Susan, the receptionist, smiled at us when we walked into the room.

"Your mother is waiting in her room," she said.

I wrote our names on two name tags and signed into the facility. Mom had lived here since her brain aneurysm four years ago. She refused to let me drop out of college to take care of her back home, telling me that I should live my life, get a job and an education, be free and independent—even if it was just for four years.

When I put the pen down, Susan took my hand. "She's not doing good today. Physical therapy was difficult for her, and ... and she needs a good smile."

Mason snatched my hand and pulled me down the hallway toward Mom's room. The light in her room was off, but her television was on, playing a rerun of *Full House*.

Mason knocked on the door and tugged me into the room, turning the light on. "Ms. Stevenson?"

"Mason, is that you?" she asked, squinting. She lay in the bed, her brown hair looking like it hadn't been brushed all weekend, her bright brown eyes wide in delight.

I sighed and closed the door behind us, grabbing her comb from the counter. "Mom, are they taking care of you here?"

She maneuvered herself into a sitting position with her arms and plastered a smile on her face, giving me that look she always did right before she told me, "It's fine, sweetheart. They're treating me great."

Mason took the comb from me and gestured to Mom to sit up even more. He sat behind her, glancing at me. I could tell by the look on his face that he actually agreed with me for once that they weren't taking good enough care of her.

He pushed it through her hair carefully. "I can find you a place that treats you better, Ms. S."

Mom laughed, and I almost rolled my eyes. Jeez, they got along better than we did.

She smiled weakly at the ground. "Don't be silly. You've done too much for me and Mia. This"—she gestured to the room around us—"and having Mia stay with you while I'm here … it's more than I could ask for."

I frowned, wrapping my arms around my body and staring at the ground. A rush of guilt washed over me as I thought about what I had done this past weekend with Mr. Bryne. If Mom found out about it … hell, if she found out that Mason and I had been … *fighting*—and I said that lightly because it wasn't really fighting, more like annoying the living daylights out of each other—she wouldn't be happy. She'd worry, and I didn't need her worrying at all.

I needed her to get better because I was in the midst of saving up enough money to get an apartment of my own so that I could care for her.

I grabbed her wheelchair from the corner of the room and brought it to her bed. "How about some time outside?"

"After you're done with your hair," Mason said, cutting in before Mom had a chance to even speak.

He narrowed his eyes at me from behind Mom's back, and I waited *patiently* for him to finish brushing her hair even though he had already gotten out all the knots.

When he finished, I grabbed it from him and watched him lift Mom and place her into the chair. We walked outside in the sun, talking about the garden and all the memories of when I had been younger. It was what we talked about every day. That was, until Mom brought up my girls' weekend.

I stared at the concrete sidewalks, avoiding all eye contact with Mason. *Don't think of Mr. Bryne. Don't mention Mr. Bryne. Act like Mr. Bryne doesn't exist, Mia.*

"I went into the pool." I fiddled with the ends of my sleeves. Mom and Mason didn't say anything for a long time, and I felt like *I* needed to fill the silence with something. "Mr. Bryne was there too."

When the words left my mouth, I nearly slapped a hand over my forehead. Mom smiled in the sun and sat back in her seat, closing her eyes.

"How is he?" she asked. "I hope he's doing well. I haven't seen him since you went off to college."

"He's doing ... well." Really goddamn well.

"Good," she said.

We walked around for a few more minutes until a nurse called for Mom to come back inside because she had another rehabilitation session.

"I have a speech session in a few minutes."

Mason wheeled her back into the building, and a nurse grabbed the handles of her wheelchair from him.

I pulled Mom into a tight hug and smiled. "Hopefully, I'll be able to stop by tomorrow."

"Please do," she said. "But if you're busy, don't worry about it."

She pulled Mason into a hug next, and then she disappeared down the hall with a nurse. I frowned at her departing figure, wishing that I could still live with her, wishing that Dad hadn't left her without any money, that she and I were back in the old house, creating a new life together. But like Dad ... that house and our old life were gone.

CHAPTER 8

MIA

When we got home, Mason was buzzed.

He pushed me into our bedroom, his hands all over my body. "Come on, baby. Let's have some fun."

He pulled up the back of my dress, pressing his cock into my backside, his nose grazing against my soft spot. I sighed to myself and let him bend me over the bed.

Within a few moments, he had hiked my dress all the way up, taken out his cock, and thrust it into me, pounding away, not caring that my fingers were digging into his thighs because he hadn't even tried foreplay and my pussy was dry yet again.

"Your pussy's always so tight for me, baby."

"Mason," I whispered, squeezing my eyes closed and trying to get wet. When I closed my eyes, all I could see was Mr. Bryne, all I could feel was Mr. Bryne, and I clenched.

"You like that, don't you?"

I took a deep breath. "Mason, it stings."

He grabbed a fistful of my hair and leaned over me, placing his lips on my neck. "Hmm?" he asked, voice terrifyingly low.

I didn't know if he'd heard me or if he was playing games with me.

"Harder," I whispered, not wanting to piss off a drunk Mason. "Please."

Mason rammed into me, and I tried to imagine his hands as Mr. Bryne's—though I'd promised myself that I wouldn't, it still happened. I wanted to imagine his lips running up my back, his fingers dipping between my legs, his cock swelling inside of me.

But Mason felt nothing like Mr. Bryne. Mason felt like a wannabe frat boy in high school who didn't know the clit from the G-spot, that kid who told everyone that he had slept with a bazillion girls before but had barely even touched a breast. It was sloppy and too rough and, honestly, pretty damn terrible.

"Please come for me," I said into the mattress, my voice monotone.

Mason grunted above me and came. When he pulled himself out, he rolled onto the bed next to me. I crawled onto the bed, wanting so desperately to give him another chance, wanting him to make me come. Hell, I *needed* him to at least try.

After my little run-in with Mr. Bryne ... I was getting so desperate for Mason to please me.

So, I turned onto my side and said, "Do you want to help me come?" I curled my fingers around his. "Please."

He took a deep breath, glancing at me. "You didn't come?"

"No."

He sighed through his nose. "Fine."

He pushed a hand between my legs, but I grabbed it, sucking his fingers into my mouth before they touched my dry pussy. He pushed them around in circles around my clit. And I closed my eyes and sank into the bedsheets, thinking about how good I was feeling.

My back arched lightly, and I moaned to myself. "Oh God ..."

I clutched the bedsheets, my body on the verge of coming when he suddenly started to move his fingers around slower, ruining the rhythm. And then his fingers stopped moving altogether.

I looked over at him to see his eyes closed and drool falling from his lower lip. I closed my eyes, pushed his hand off of me, and pulled the blankets over my body, turning away from him. Even when I gave him a chance ... he had to ruin it.

* * *

"Do you want to go out?" Mason asked me on Thursday night.

I stared up at him from the bed and watched him walk into the bedroom, a towel wrapped around his waist, beads of water dripping down his taut chest.

Out? Mason wants to go ... out? Between school and work and seeing Mom, we hadn't been out on a date in weeks.

He dropped his towel in the middle of the room, not caring that he was getting everything wet. "Huh?" he asked me, giving me that *are you going to answer or just stare at me* look in the mirror.

My eyes widened, and I sat up. "Yeah, let's go."

Mason finally wanted to go out on a date, and I wasn't about to pass up this opportunity. Tonight would be a good time to chill out and relax, to spend some quality time with him, and to *not* think about ... Mr. Bryne. Because I hadn't been thinking about anyone else but Mr. Bryne for the past few days. Every day was getting worse and worse.

"Well, don't just sit there." Mason tugged a dress shirt over his head. "Get ready."

I pursed my lips together and ignored his remark, walking toward my closet and finding my favorite navy-colored wrap-around dress.

"Don't you want to wear that red dress I got you?" Mason asked. "You wear that dress every time we go out."

Bite your tongue. Don't let him get to your head. You owe him so damn much.

"I like this dress," I said, smoothing out the material and taking a deep breath. I slung my purse over my shoulder and smiled at him. "I'm ready."

* * *

MASON BROUGHT me to this upscale bar down in the city. I had never been there, but it seemed like he had—many times. The waitresses and bartenders greeted him as they would an old friend. I glanced at all the women who were looking him up and down, pushing out their breasts, unbuttoning a couple buttons of their shirts, and nearly rolled my eyes. God, some of these people were beyond desperate.

"Mason," I said, grabbing his hand and inching close to him. "Are you sure this is okay?"

I didn't care that we had come here, but part of me felt bad. This place looked way, way, way out of my budget, and … I was feeling beyond guilty for letting Mason pay for everything with his parents' money—from Mom's living arrangements to all the bills to taking me out to dinner. All I paid for was Mom's therapy and some of my college. Nothing for him.

"It's fine." He slid onto a seat at the far end of the bar and held two fingers up toward the bartender. "Two menus."

She sauntered over to us, placed the menus on the bar, and smiled sweetly at Mason, flicking a strand of her awfully dyed red hair out of her face. "It's nice to see you again, Mason."

I grabbed the menu from her and buried my face into it, deciding not to listen to Mason say anything to her. It wasn't any of my damn business what he was saying to her, especially after what *I* had done with Mr. Bryne.

A few moments later, she placed two drinks on the bar in front of us. I grabbed my sangria and drank it down faster than I ever had. Maybe it'd give me the buzz I needed to ask Mason for another favor—to move Mom to a better assisted living home.

But after I finished the entire drink, I still didn't say a word. At least Mom was there. She could be somewhere worse. Hell, if it wasn't for Mason, we could be living on the side of the road with no money to our name.

I tapped my fingers on my glass, watching Mason text on his phone from the corner of my eye. So much for going out on a nice date. I glanced up and—

Mr. Bryne sat with a young woman across the bar. His body was turned toward hers, his arm around the back of her chair. He leaned in and smiled.

Something inside of me stirred, and I tightened my palm around my glass until my knuckles turned white. Mr. Bryne said something to her, and she laughed, her nose scrunching up, her fingers brushing against his chest.

I pursed my lips together. Who was—

No, no ... I didn't care. I didn't care who she was. What had happened between Mr. Bryne and me was a one-time thing, never to be mentioned or thought about again.

"Mason," I said, trying so desperately to pull my attention away from Mr. Bryne and whoever he was out on a date with. "Do you want to ..."

"To?" he asked, barely looking in my direction. The waitress sauntered over again, and he looked up from his phone with a big smile. "Two more, and let's do a side of chicken tacos."

She took our menus away, and he went back to texting on his damn phone. I slumped down in my seat, kept my eyes on the table, and frowned. He had asked me out on a date and then wasn't paying attention to me at all. *Great.*

I was stuck with him on a stale date while Mr. Bryne was over there with some pretty girl, laughing and having the time of his life.

"Mason!" someone shouted from across the bar.

I glanced up to see one of his friends. I didn't know his name. Mason knew way too many people for me to keep track of. They did that weird guy hug, clapping their hands together. After giving him my best smile, I watched him slide into the seat next to Mason and listened to them start talking about the party the other night.

My gaze drifted to Mr. Bryne. His arm was still around the woman's chair, but he was sipping his drink and gazing over at *me*.

CHAPTER 9

MIA

As soon as I made eye contact with him, I pulled my gaze away, my heart pounding against my chest.

God, I hated this. What was wrong with me? Why was I feeling this way about my best friend's dad when I was sitting next to Mason, my boyfriend who had done everything for me? Why was I ... jealous?

The woman stood up, leaving her purse on the bar next to him, and walked toward the restroom. When she disappeared, he glanced back at me, and I looked away. Maybe I felt jealous because unlike *me*, she was at least getting some attention from a man.

The slutty bartender—yes, I'd decided she was slutty—placed a glass of wine on the bar in front of me.

Mason looked over, scowling. "What's this?" he asked her. "She didn't order wine."

"Compliments of the gentleman over there."

Mason glanced over across the bar with his jaw taut, but when he saw Melissa's father, his hard expression fell. "It's just Melissa's dad," he said, nodding to him, then turning back to his friend.

That was all this man had to fucking say? "It's just Melissa's dad." Not, Why is Melissa's dad trying to get you drunk? Why is Melissa's dad ordering you a drink? Why is Melissa's dad staring at you with those deep, gray eyes?

I took a deep breath and looked back at Mr. Bryne, picking up my glass and sipping it. He leaned forward, forearms on the bar, and parted his lips, as if he would say something, but then that stupid brunette came back and sat next to him, her fingers dipping to his forearm.

He leaned closer to her and whispered something into her ear, and she nodded to him. He stood up, glanced at me from over her shoulder, and headed toward the restroom.

Instead of sitting next to Mason and listening to him rave about Saturday night, I told him that I needed to use the restroom and followed Mr. Bryne down the hallway.

"Following me, Mia?" he asked, turning around, brow arched.

"How's your date?" I asked him through gritted teeth, waiting by the restroom door.

"Better than yours."

I pursed my lips and peered back into the bar to see that waitress leaning over the counter and talking to Mason again. My heart ached, and I shook my head.

"Good," I said, deciding that coming back here was wrong. I should've stayed in the damn seat and listened to the frat-boy conversation between the annoying asshole and the annoying asshole's friend.

I pushed the restroom door open, but Mr. Bryne snatched my wrist and pulled me back. "Where do you think you're going?"

"To use the bathroom."

He pulled me back out into the small hallway and took a step closer to me. "We both know that's not why you followed me."

I raised a brow at him, trying to keep myself calm. "And why do you think I followed you?"

He smirked, his fingers running up my sides. "How's Mason doing?" he asked, leaning down, his nose brushing against my neck.

I shivered and placed my hands firmly against his chest, but I didn't push him away. His hands roamed my body, falling lower and lower until he was squeezing my ass.

"He's doing fine."

"Fine?" he asked, chuckling in my ear.

I could feel my nipples stiffen against my bra, and all I could think about were his lips all over my breasts last weekend, kissing, sucking, biting every part of me.

"He treats you—"

"Fine. He treats me fine." I gathered all my strength and pushed him away, glancing over at Mason, who was flirting with that woman.

God, it was awful to stay with him after what I had done ... but he had done so much for Mom. Without him, I'd have to drop out of college—and I was so close to finishing—just to pay the bills, and even then, the prices in the city were too high to live off of a single shitty income.

I pursed my lips together and glanced at my feet. "You know what?" I turned away, about to walk back down the hallway. "Don't talk to—"

He seized my wrist again, pulling me close to him until our bodies were nearly pressing together. He set his arm around my waist, his fingers dancing on my lower back. "I like this dress on you."

My breath caught in my throat, a weird feeling spreading through my body. It was a feeling that I should have never ever felt for my best friend's father.

He smirked against my neck, his stubble grazing against it and making me shiver. I took a deep breath, listening to Mason's voice in the bar, chuckling with that woman.

I yanked myself out of Mr. Bryne's grasp, reluctantly stepped away, and looked him up and down. "What happened between us was a one-time thing. It won't happen again."

But, boy, was I wrong.

CHAPTER 10

MIA

"Her dad is so fucking hot," one of the sorority girls said, lowering her sunglasses and staring at Mr. Bryne.

Melissa was throwing the biggest end-of-the-summer party that I had ever seen with nearly a hundred people at her father's house—mostly guys and some girls from our college. And of course, Mr. Bryne was here, as it was his day off of work.

Something about the way that chick had said it made me clench my jaw. I didn't know what it was because I definitely —*definitely*—didn't care about Mr. Bryne like that. He was just my best friend's dad, just a guy I'd fucked, just a man I thought about when I needed something to get me off.

Nothing more.

And he would never be anything more.

I would spend the rest of my life with Mason.

Only Mason.

I took a deep breath and watched her adjust her tiny bikini, which showed way too much boob, if you asked me. But, hey, I didn't care. Not one fucking bit.

She put her glasses back on and smiled at the other girls around her. "The things I would do to sleep with him." She bit her fake lip and threw her head back, overexaggerating every single thing she did. Probably to get his attention.

I turned away and stared at the guys in the pool. How were cliché girls really real? I'd thought they were just in the damn books and movies, but this chick ... God, this chick ...

I wanted to wrap my hands around her throat and squ—

Mason sat up from the pool chair, put his glasses down on the bench next to me, and smiled. For the first time today, he ruffled my hair—showing the first sign of affection—and placed his lips on my forehead, kissing me. "You want me to put some lotion on you?" he asked. "You're burning."

I gazed at him, taken aback, but then I scooted to the edge of the pool chair and handed him the sunscreen. I wasn't going to say no. I didn't need to say no. I had nothing to prove. Mason grabbed it from me and squirted some onto his hand, sitting behind me to rub it on my back. His fingers got dangerously close to the strings of my bikini, slipping under the material.

For a moment, I relaxed under his fingers ...

See, Mason can be a sweetheart when he want—

"All the guys are looking at you," he said in that jealous tone he always had.

When we'd first started dating, I'd thought that his possessiveness was sexy, but his possessiveness turned him into a monster. A guy would look at me, and this man thought *I* wanted to fuck *him*.

"It's nothing, Mason. Don't even worry about them."

He continued putting the sunscreen on my back, and I stayed tense the whole time, knowing that the only reason he was doing it was to let everyone else know that I was his and not anyone else's.

He wasn't doing it because I was burning. He wasn't doing it because he cared. He was doing it for himself.

When he finished, I turned onto my stomach and buried my face into the cushions of the pool chair. All I wanted was someone who put as much effort into me as I put into them, someone who put me first, who treated me with respect, who wanted to please *me*.

"You think if I flirted hard enough, he'd want to fuck me?" the sorority girl said, walking by me and swaying her hips from side to side.

I closed my eyes. *No, bitch, he wouldn't.*

* * *

I CLIMBED out of the pool through the ladder as water rolled down my breasts. We had been out in the sun for nearly three hours, and all Mr. Bryne had been doing was tanning. At one point, he had taken a dip in the water, and I swore all our friends and the sorority girls had drooled over him.

I supposed that some would even try to flirt with him later, but I didn't care. Nope. Not one bit because I was here with Mason, my *lovely* boyfriend.

I dried myself off with a beach towel and tossed it next to Mason, who was on his phone. He had barely given me the time of day today, and he had jumped in Mr. Bryne's pool once to play with some of the guys that Melissa had over.

Mr. Bryne was on the other side of the pool, lying on his back, beads of sweat rolling down his abdomen. I looked over at him for a moment, wondering if he was staring at me through his dark sunglasses, then looked back to Melissa.

"I'm going to get something to drink," I said. "I'll be back."

Wine. I needed more wine. I needed it to think clearly because all I could think about was *him*, even when my boyfriend was right next to me. I snuck Mr. Bryne one more quick glance and walked into the house through the back door.

My pussy was warm, and I had the urge to take Mason to the bathroom in an attempt to feel kind of good. It wouldn't be as good as Mr. Bryne, but nothing would ever be that good.

In the upstairs kitchen by myself, I popped the cork on a bottle of white wine and poured myself a glass.

Mr. Bryne walked into the kitchen, grabbed a glass from inside one of the cupboards next to me, and took the bottle from my hand. "Didn't expect to see Mason here today, Mia." He put the cork back into the bottle and grabbed his glass, his fingers paling.

"I didn't expect to see you, Mr. Bryne."

He tilted his head, his sharp, piercing eyes cutting right through me. "Yes, you did." He curled one finger under my bikini string and tugged. "That's why you wore this tiny little bikini today."

When he released the string, it hit my chest, and my tits bounced with it. He eyed them for a long moment.

"Is that why you followed me upstairs?" I asked, arching a brow and walking toward the living room. The living room had a large glass door that led out to a stair-less deck that overlooked the pool. From here, I could see everyone—from Mason to Melissa to all the other guys she had invited over to have a good time with after she broke up with her boyfriend.

"Oh, Mia." He shook his head and stared out the window next to me. "That's why you came up here, isn't it?" He placed his full lips on his glass, and all I could remember were those same lips on my clit, eating me until my legs were trembling around him. "You wanted me to follow you up here because Mason is utterly useless when it comes to pleasing you."

"He's not useless," I said, looking away.

Mason was lying out by the pool, still texting on his phone, completely oblivious to me being gone. Okay, he was useless.

"How many times has he made you come since the other night?"

I placed my glass on a side table and crossed my arms over my chest. "The other night that you are referring to was over a week ago." And, yes, I had been thinking about him every time I finished myself off after Mason and I had sex. It was beyond wrong, but ... I couldn't help myself.

"So, he hasn't at all." He took another sip of his wine and nodded, his muscles rippling. "Didn't expect a big performance from him."

I turned around on my heel, looking directly at him for the first time since we had made it upstairs. God, how the fuck was his body so nice? He was Melissa's father, for fuck's sake; he shouldn't look like—

He smirked down at me and nodded to the window. I turned back, gazing outside at Mason, and felt his body heat so much closer to mine.

"Maybe ..." His fingers grazed against my hip. "Maybe I should show Mason how to please you."

"No," I said, trying to keep my breathing steady. "We can't do it again."

"It wouldn't take long to get you screaming."

"Mr. Bryne, we can't."

He tugged on the bottom string of my bikini top. It came undone, and my tits bounced out of it. "Oops."

I grabbed the string, desperate to tie it before anyone saw. "Oops? Oops? That's all you have to say?"

Mr. Bryne undid the top string and let it fall completely down. He stepped closer to me. "Why don't you take it off, Mia?" He took the bottom string from my hand and tugged on it once again, undoing everything I had just done to keep myself covered. "You look better without it."

In one swoop, he tore the bikini off of me and tossed it to the side. Then, he pushed my body against the glass door, making me press my breasts into it. "Mia, on display for all of her friends to see." He smirked against my neck. "Too bad it's still daylight. Your boyfriend can't actually see into the window and see what a good time really looks like."

"Mr. Bryne … they can still …" I closed my eyes when he plunged his fingers into my bikini bottoms.

"They can still what?"

"Still … see …" I said quietly.

He skimmed his nose against my ear, fingers moving in quick circles. "They won't be able to see you, Mia … but that doesn't mean they won't be able to hear every time I make you scream." He cupped my chin in his hand and roughly brushed his thumb over my bottom lip.

I didn't believe it. I didn't believe it one bit. They would see me, *and* they would hear me.

Standing naked in front of a glass door, staring down at all of my friends and boyfriend, being fucked by Mr. Bryne … God, it was fucking wrong … but I hadn't stopped thinking about last time.

When he spilled water all over my tiny white tank top so he could finally see my tits. When he thrust into my pussy as his daughter and my best friend walked right into the room. When he made me come so many times that I lost count.

"Your pussy is getting so wet for me," he said. He pushed his hips against mine from behind, letting me feel his stiffness poking through his swim trunks. "How many times have you touched your pussy while thinking about me?"

He slid his finger between my folds and pushed it inside. I whimpered, clenching on his fingers.

"How many times, Mia?"

"None."

His fingers moved faster inside of me, pumping in and out of my pussy wildly. He grabbed my hand and placed it on his cock behind me. I gripped him through his shorts, moving my hand up and down.

"You haven't thought about my cock inside of you?"

Oh, God, help me.

Everyone outside was splashing around in the water and relaxing, and here I was, getting finger-fucked by my best friend's dad.

Heat warmed my pussy, and I tightened on him. So close to coming undone.

"Once? Twice?"

He groped one of my breasts and took my nipple in between two of his fingers, tugging on it harshly. Delight rolled through me, and I moaned.

"Every night," I whispered, moving my hand up and down his length. "Every fucking night, Mr. Bryne."

"There you go." He nibbled on my jaw. "That wasn't so hard to admit, was it?"

I placed my fingertips on the glass, staring out at everyone who could look up at the deck at any moment and see us through the glass, see him touching me like this. "But we can't do it."

"If you don't want to do it again, Mia, we won't."

Mr. Bryne pushed my bikini bottoms down my legs and parted my thighs. I pushed my hand into his swim trunks, my wet pussy pulsing.

"We'll walk back out to the pool, like nothing happened."

I nodded. "Yeah." I pulled his cock out of his bottoms and stroked it against my ass. "Like nothing happened."

He drew his fingers up the insides of my thighs and spread my legs further apart. "You can go back to Mason and have him continue to *pleasure* you every night."

"I will," I said, pushing my hips against his.

"You won't have to feel this …"

He grabbed his cock in his hand and set it against my pussy lips. I clenched, waiting for him to enter me. He pinched my nipple in his fingers, and another wave of ecstasy rolled through me.

"Or this." Then, he plunged himself inside of me.

My body shuddered in pure ecstasy. "Never … want … to feel that … again."

He stilled inside of me, grabbing on to one of my shoulders and pushing me further down onto his cock until all of it was inside of me. "Fuck," he groaned against my ear.

I moved my hips back and forth on him, unable to stop myself. "Mason fucks me so much better than you ever could."

He seized my hips and started to drive himself in and out of me faster. "I bet he does." One of his hands slipped to my clit, and he began rubbing it harshly.

"The way he tugs on my nipples …"

Mr. Bryne took one of my nipples between his fingers.

"The way he slaps my clit with his hand."

Mr. Bryne slapped his hand against my clit, and my body jerked into the air. Heat warmed my core. I gripped his cock harder, loving how big he felt inside of me. Mason never ever felt this good.

"What about the way he makes you scream?" he asked me, shoving me against the glass window, ramming up into me, making my legs tremble.

He snaked a hand around my throat, and I pressed my lips together and tried not to scream. If I did … someone would hear me, and then …

He slapped my clit again.

And I screamed, unable to hold myself back any longer as he continued to plunge his huge cock into my pussy. Pure ecstasy was pumping through me as I came almost instantly on him.

He snaked one arm around my neck, pulling me closer to him, and placed his other hand on the small of my back to keep it curved. My tits bounced against the glass.

Downstairs, the back door opened, and I listened to someone walk into the house. I tensed and reached back for Mr. Bryne, hoping he'd stop. But he continued pounding into me faster.

"Mia!" Melissa shouted. "Is everything okay? We heard you scream."

My eyes widened. *What do I say to that? Can I even open my mouth without moaning her father's name? What if—*

"She's fine. Just dropped some glass," Mr. Bryne said.

"Dropped glass? Oh my gosh, is she okay?"

Mr. Bryne growled into my ear, and my pussy tightened around him. He gripped my hips, slowed his pace, and thrust deep.

"She's fine, Melissa. She'll be out soon."

I grabbed my bikini in case I needed to put it on really quick and tightened around him. I was so close to the edge, so close to moaning out his name so loud that everyone could hear, so close to coming again.

"Go back to your friends."

"Are you sure?"

"Yes," he said, his tone tenser than before.

The back door opened and closed again, and Mr. Bryne picked me up right off the ground—his cock still inside of me—and walked with me to his bedroom. Though I had never been inside of it before, he didn't give me any time to look around and admire it. Instead, he bent me right over the bed, pushed my face into the mattress, and continued to pump into me.

"How long will it take her to figure out that you're not coming back out until I'm finished fucking your tight little pussy?"

My pussy clenched on him, and I groaned into the bedsheets. "I-I—"

He grabbed a fistful of my hair and pulled my upper body off of the bed. After pressing his lips on my neck, he sucked roughly on the skin underneath it. He pumped into me, each stroke sending me closer and closer to the bed. His hand wrapped around my neck, and he squeezed lightly.

Wave after wave of pleasure rolled through me. I grasped the bedsheets and moaned loudly, not caring who could hear me anymore. All I knew was, this was orgasm two, and there was bound to be more.

After pounding into me one last time, he pulled out, turned me around, and forced me onto my knees. "Fuck, Mia, hold those tits together for me."

He stroked his cock in my face, and I pushed my tits together for him to come on.

"Open your mouth," he said, groaning.

I gazed up at him, opened my mouth, and stuck out my tongue.

He drew his brows together and looked down at my tits. He slid his cock between them, pushing up and down. I stared at his cock, tugging on my nipples and moaning.

"Eyes up here, Mia."

I glanced up at him. He parted his lips, legs trembling, and came between my tits. He groaned, the last of his cum dripping out onto me, and then he reached down, picked me up, and tossed me onto his bed.

He crawled onto the bed with me, parting my trembling legs, and sat between them. "You don't know how long I've waited to see you in my bed …" He swept two fingers against his cum on my chest and stuck them into my mouth, and I sucked the cum off of them. "Swallowing my cum." He leaned down between my legs and pressed his lips to my clit. "Eating your tight little pussy again."

After he placed my legs on his thighs, he reached up, seized my nipples, and tugged on them. His tongue massaged my clit in fast circles. I furrowed my brows and grabbed on to his wrists, loving the way he touched me.

When he squeezed my nipples harder, I screamed out, my legs trembling. He continued to eat me until I came down from orgasm three of the day, and then he sat up between my legs and watched me. Then he finally said, "Dump Mason."

CHAPTER 11

MIA

I gulped, trying to think about something other than the mind-numbing orgasms I'd had. "But—"

"Dump Mason, and I'll make you come like this every night."

Dump Mason. Dump Mason. Dump Mason.

I couldn't get the words out of my head. I didn't want to get the words out of my head. I had been thinking about it for such a long time now, but when Mr. Bryne had said it out loud … it made it real somehow. And I didn't like the way I felt about it … because it wasn't just me that I had to look out for. It was Mom too.

He gazed down at me with those pretty gray eyes that I could get lost in forever, and I didn't want to stop staring into them. But I knew that I had to stop. I had to stop this, whatever the hell this was.

"I can't." I forced the words out of my mouth. Tried to convince myself that this was what I really wanted. Promised myself that when I got a good job and could support Mom … I'd dump Mason. But I didn't know if I'd ever be able to support Mom with all her medical bills; I didn't know if I'd ever be able to afford a caretaker for her when I had to work.

Mr. Bryne placed his hands on my knees and clenched his jaw. "You can, Mia," he said, voice dangerously low. His soft eyes turned hard, and all that playfulness in them completely disappeared.

"I can't stop seeing him, nor will I."

He shook his head at me, brows drawn down in anger. "He treats you like garbage. He barely acknowledges you. He flirts with other women right fucking in front of you."

I scrambled to sit up in the bed and then leaped off of it, searching through his drawers for something to cover my body so I didn't go prancing through his house, naked.

God, I didn't need to hear this right now. I knew what Mason did. I knew why he did it. I knew that he was a shit person … but so was I for using him. Maybe we were good for each other in that way.

He hopped off the bed and snatched my wrist before I could open the door and leave. "Is that really how you want to be treated for the rest of your life, Mia?"

After yanking myself out of his hold, I stared up at him. "What else am I supposed to do?" I asked, pure rage rushing through me. It wasn't like I had a fucking choice. Either deal with Mason or live on the fucking streets and watch Mom get thrown into another terrible facility.

"You're acting as if you don't have a choice."

My jaw twitched. "So, I dump him, so I can fuck you whenever I want?" I shook my head and grabbed the door handle again. "I can't do that. You don't understand."

"Enlighten me then." He grasped my wrist and pulled me back again so I faced him. Completely naked, muscles swollen, eyes so damn intense that I had to remind myself that I shouldn't be feeling this way. "What don't I understand about being treated like shit? It's only going to get worse from here." He sounded like he was speaking from experience. "I'm trying to help you."

All I wanted to do was tell him about everything I had been through these past few years ... cry my eyes out like I had every night that first year after Mom had her accident. I wanted him to tell me that it was all going to be okay, that Mom would get better, that she was happy in a place that treated her so poorly.

But I couldn't *enlighten* him about my situation. I couldn't tell him that the only damn reason I was still in this relationship with Mason was because of Mom. I didn't want him to think of me as a gold-digger. I didn't ask Mason to buy me things or take me places. I just ... I wanted a place to live and for Mom to be safe.

That was all. But I was terrified that Mr. Bryne wouldn't see it that way, and I wanted him to see me how I was, for him to treat me normally. I didn't need his pity.

"What is holding you back?" he asked, shaking his head.

My eyes filled with tears that I promised myself wouldn't fall. All I wanted was for Mom to be happy. After everything that had happened with Dad ... she deserved more than happiness. And if I had to endure a shitty life to see her smile, then I would. I couldn't let this little obsession with my best friend's father get in the way.

Mr. Bryne's eyes softened, and then he brushed his finger over a strand of hair that had fallen into my face. It was a subtle gesture, but it was more affection than Mason had given me in such a long time.

"Mia," he said, voice low, "talk to me."

I wrapped my arms around myself and turned away before my tears fell. "This is a mistake," I whispered, opening his bedroom door and walking right out of the room. "We are a mistake."

CHAPTER 12

MICHAEL

It took everything I had not to follow her as she stormed down the hallway, wearing my shirt that barely covered her ass. She disappeared into the bathroom, fumbled around in it, and then came out in her tiny white bikini that I wanted to tear off again, and with a bandage that she slapped right on her thigh to hide the fact that she hadn't actually gotten cut by glass.

When she disappeared down the stairs, I placed my hands on the doorframe and took a few deep breaths, trying to control myself. Something kept her from breaking up with Mason. She saw what I saw—that her boyfriend didn't give a single fuck about her—but she stayed with him. Wouldn't even consider breaking up with him.

What was it, though?

I glanced at my dresser, memories of years ago haunting my mind. Was he abusing her? She didn't have bruises or scars, but she had fear in those deep brown eyes of hers.

The phone on my dresser buzzed. Almost as if the devil knew I had been thinking about her, Linda's name flashed on the screen.

I picked up the phone, jaw twitching. "The next time you call me, I'm blocking your fucking number." The only reason I hadn't already was because of Melissa. Whenever she did go to her mom's place, which wasn't often, I needed a way to get hold of her in case something happened. Melissa was terrible at responding to texts. "What do you want?"

"You haven't let Melissa throw another one of those end-of-year parties, have you?" she asked, acting like she cared. "You know she needs to study and work. She'd better not be drinking. She's underage."

"She's twenty-two, Linda."

"Still." She paused. "She should be stud-y-ing."

I pursed my lips. She was drunk again, like she had been almost every day we were married. I blew a deep breath out of my nose.

"You don't care about Melissa that much to check up on her anymore," I said through gritted teeth. "What do you really want?"

She stayed quiet for a few moments, and I could hear her tapping her fake nails against a table. "I heard you went out on a date the other night."

There it was. There was always something.

"What's her name?"

"That's none of your business."

"Her name's Julie, isn't it?" She chuckled and swallowed loud enough for me to hear. "She's young and so pretty. Way out of your league. You should get back together with that piece of trailer trash you were dating a few years ago. You know, the one with the bad tit job. She's more your type."

"Why don't you care about Melissa anymore?" I asked, so desperate to know why.

All I had ever wanted since our divorce was for her to treat Melissa well. Every time I picked up the phone, I wanted her to ask about Melissa and really fucking care. She wasn't the same woman she had been when I married her.

"But ... I heard the trailer trash cheated on you. Is that right?" She laughed again. "Guess that's all you're good for—"

I hung up the phone and rubbed my forehead, not about to deal with another second of her putting me down.

My phone buzzed again in my hand, and I almost threw it across the room. But a text message popped up on the screen. Linda never texted me. I glanced down at it, seeing Julie's name on the screen.

Julie: Wanna come over tonight? I'm making your favorite—grilled oysters. ;)

I took a deep breath, my fingers hovering over the keyboard, and gazed out my bedroom window, watching Mia lay on her pool chair, rubbing sunscreen on her pale chest. She looked absolutely miserable as she watched Mason in the pool with some of the other girls.

When she glanced up at the house, I backed away and took a deep breath, trying hard not to think about her back in my bed, her pussy tightening around my cock, her back arching, her lips parted ever so slightly. Her eyes lighting up when she had seen me from across the bar the other night, the way her head had tilted into my hand when I pushed a strand of hair from her face, the way *my* heart had raced when she smiled.

God, it was wrong, so fucking wrong. She was my daughter's best friend. I shouldn't have touched her, never mind ... felt like *this*.

Me: Rain check? I have plans with my daughter tonight.

To my surprise, Julie didn't text back as quickly as she usually did. I placed the phone back onto the dresser and walked back down the stairs and out to the pool.

The only plan I had tonight was with Mia.

CHAPTER 13

MIA

I stared at Mr. Bryne from across the yard. After what had happened in his bedroom, I tried to avoid him at all costs. But Mason wanted to stay at this party all night, and Melissa begged me to stay over, so all chances of avoiding him kind of went right out the window.

Shirt off, towel hanging off his shoulder, he stood by the grill and aimlessly flipped burgers, looking as if he was lost in his own little world. Some girls from the sorority stood by him, their tits hanging out of their stupid little bikinis as they talked to him. I clenched my jaw and pulled out my phone, texting Mom.

Me: Hope you're doing all right. I'll come see you tomorrow.

She texted back a few moments later.

Mom: Can't wait to see you. Love you with everything.

I smiled, and then another text came through.

Mom: Is Mason coming?

I glanced over at Mason, sitting by Melissa and some of the other guys from his frat.

Me: No.

Mom sent me a frowny-face emoji, and *my* frown deepened. *God, why do I feel like this? Why can't I love Mason and think he's the most perfect person in the entire world?*

"Mia," Melissa shouted from the firepit. She shoved a hot dog on a stick into the fire.

I took a deep breath and sank further into the cushioned seat.

Why couldn't Mason care about *me* the way he used to? We used to go on so many dates. He used to buy me flowers, create cute playlists to show how he felt about me. Hell, I'd appreciate a text every now and then.

"Mia," Melissa said, hopping onto a seat next to me.

I pressed a hand to my chest, feeling startled, and stared at her, face void of any emotion.

She nodded to everyone now cuddling up near the fire and eating. "Come on. We're playing Truth or Dare—*not safe for work* edition."

"Melissa …" I sighed through my nose and threw my head back, staring up at the stars. "I'm not really feeling it right now."

She sat up. "What's wrong?"

"Nothing."

"Oh, don't give me that."

"It's nothing," I said again, glancing at Mason. I frowned, partly because of the guilt and partly because I didn't want to spend my life with someone who barely paid attention to me. *Stupid Mr. Bryne putting stupid thoughts in my head about stupid Mason.*

Melissa followed my gaze. "I told you to dump him," she said yet again. Then, she winked at me. "Or … if you like him for his mon—"

"I don't like him for the money."

She raised a brow at me. "You can always have a little fun on the side."

I gulped and closed my eyes. I never wanted to cheat. I really, really never did. I hated the guilt and the lies and the feeling of being exactly like my father.

"That's what I do," she said.

I stared at her with wide eyes. She had said it with such ... with such ... a lack of remorse, like cheating on her boyfriend didn't make her feel guilty. Hell, I didn't even know that they had gotten back together. When on earth did that happen? And when did she cheat on him? Did he even know?

She laughed and grabbed my hand, trying to pull me to my feet. "I'm kidding, Mia. I wanted to get you to smile."

I yanked my hand out of hers, anger pumping through me, and sank back into the cushion. "Melissa, I'll be over there later."

She shrugged her shoulders and walked back to her father, telling him something. Mr. Bryne closed the grill and glanced over at me, holding a plate of food. I looked away from him and stared at my toes, wiggling them.

What is wrong with me? Why am I even letting him get into my head?

"Take it off!" one of the guys yelled.

The fucking chick who had been trying to get with Mr. Bryne all night stood up, shaking her head from side to side. All of the guys, drunk off their fucking asses, cheered.

I rolled my eyes. *Jesus fucking Christ.* Were we on spring break or in high school? Playing Truth or Dare and making people strip off their clothes? It was so damn childish.

I glanced over at Mr. Bryne to see him picking up his plate of food and heading straight toward *me*.

"Don't you want to see the show?" I asked, voice dripping with anger, when he approached me. I didn't even know why it had come out that way; it just had. I crossed my arms over my chest. Maybe I wanted him to watch, so I'd have a reason to stop obsessing over him.

I could convince myself that what was going on between us would've gone on between him and any of Melissa's friends. That I wasn't special to him. That he really didn't care about me as much as it seemed like he did.

Mr. Bryne placed a plate of food down in front of me and sat in the pool chair to my right. "Eat," he said, grabbing a burger for himself.

I stared at the food, my stomach growling, and snatched a burger.

We ate in silence for a long time. I didn't dare say a word because I didn't know what to say to the one man I was trying so hard to avoid. When he finished his food, he looked over at Mason, who was doing God knew what for his dare.

"What did I tell you?" he said. "He doesn't even know that you've been here, sulking."

"I don't want to hear it." I smacked my lips closed and crossed my arms over my chest, watching fireflies light up in the darkness. "I already told you that this isn't happening anymore. We're not happening. We can't."

CHAPTER 14

MIA

I walked into the Orangegate Assisted Living foyer to a smiling Susan.

"Your mother is in therapy right now. She just started her session and probably won't finish for another half hour."

After nodding my head, I walked to Mom's room and sat in one of her spare seats. My knees bounced as I waited for the minutes to go by. This place kind of creeped me out. I had spent too many nights in the hospital, feeling so overwhelmed and anxious, for me to ever really like a place like this. So, I decided to pass the time by cleaning up.

I organized Mom's feminine products, put a new bar of soap in the shower—not that she could use it by herself—wiped down the counters, and finally grabbed the bedsheets to make the bed. But when I saw the dark stains in the middle of the sheets, I stopped and pulled back the blankets.

What the hell is this? One of the stains looked fresh while the other looked as if it had been there for days. I ripped back all the blankets and shook my head, eyes filling with tears. *How can they do this to her? Why hasn't she complained?*

I stormed out of the room and marched down the hall to Susan. "Why doesn't my mother have fresh sheets? You let her sit in her own shit? Don't help her to the bathroom when she needs to go?"

Susan's eyes widened, and she looked at some of the other patients' families. "What are you talking about?"

"There are stains on her sheets."

She stood up, blushing, and pulled me to Mom's room. When she saw them, she held her hand to her chest, drawing in a deep breath. "I'm so sorry. We'll get someone to fix it as soon as possible. We've been short-staffed lately. It won't happen again."

I stared at her and shook my head. "That's not an excuse. It shouldn't have happened at all." My jaw twitched. "I brought my mother here for you all to assist her, not for you to leave her when she needs help."

"Mia"—Susan placed her hands on my shoulders, trying to relax me—"I'm so sorry. This doesn't happen here—ever. I don't know why it happened today."

Another nurse appeared at the door, wheeling Mom into the room.

"Mia!" she said, but when she saw me, she furrowed her brows. "What's going on here?"

I took a deep breath and grabbed the handle to Mom's wheelchair to wheel her out to the garden. "Nothing. They're just cleaning up."

The sun hit my face, and I pushed her toward the garden, inhaling the scent of the tulips. I didn't want to bring up the stains to Mom because she wouldn't say a word about it—she knew that if she went somewhere else, they'd probably treat her worse—and because I didn't want to embarrass her.

She had been through so much shit this last year; I didn't want to add to it.

So, I pushed her around, talking every so often about Mason and work and the party. Anything she wanted to know about, I chatted to her about it. But ... all I could think about was that I needed to work more hours. I needed more money. I needed to find her someplace else as soon as possible.

And the worst part about this whole thing was ... I had no place to keep her until then. Mason's apartment was a one-bedroom and not handicap accessible. I didn't have as much money as I needed for an apartment or for a nurse that I trusted to work at home with us.

Things were looking bad. So damn bad. My heart ached.

After an hour in the sun together, I brought Mom back to her freshly cleaned room. The sheets had been changed, the mattress had been turned, and a new air freshener had been plugged into the wall. I helped give Mom a bath and then put her into bed, making sure she was comfortable before I left.

She grabbed my hand, squeezing it tightly, and pulled me down to place a kiss on my forehead. "I love you, Mia." Her words were gentler than usual today, and they almost made me cry. "I know you're working hard for me, and I'm sorry that I'm putting you through all this trouble."

I pushed some hair out of her face. "Mom, don't be sorry. I'd do anything for you."

She smiled at me, grasping my chin in her hand. "You look tired. When you get home, take a nap."

I smiled one last time at her, kissed her on the forehead, pulled her into a tight hug, and then I left and got on the bus, promising myself that I would get her out of there as soon as possible. I dialed my boss's number and hurried to Mason's apartment, clicking the elevator button.

My boss, Sal, answered on the first ring. "Hello?"
"Hello?"
"How do you work this damn thing?" he said, voice distant.
"Sal, can you hear me?"

"Hello! Mia, is that you?"

"Yes," I said, sighing. "I need to work more hours. I need the money. Can you put me on whenever someone drops a shift?"

"What?" Sal said again. He was about eighty years old and could barely hear, but it was the best job I'd had in a long time. "You have too many hours?"

"No, Sal," I said loudly. "I want *more* hours. Has anyone dropped any shifts?"

"Oh, yeah. Marcie just dropped one for later today!" he said, sounding happy. "Come on down. I was going to call you anyway."

I thanked the gods—whichever one it was this time—and got changed into my uniform to bartend by the river. Sunday nights were usually slow, but the job paid well. He gave me more than minimum wage, plus tips. So, I tried to go anytime I wasn't at school.

Like usual, when I got to the bar, it was dead. There were a few stragglers hanging around the tables in the back and a few regulars at the bar. I threw my hair into a high ponytail, ready for whatever shit I had to deal with tonight.

But then, halfway through my shift, the one man I didn't want to see walked right through the doors and smirked at *me*.

He didn't say anything to me throughout my whole shift. Another one of the girls waited on him, giving him a glass of wine, then a beer, then a shot of whiskey. But those eyes, those damn eyes, were fixed on me the entire night.

CHAPTER 15

MIA

"All right, Mia," Sal said, voice shrill. He walked out from the back, weakly lifting his bag and putting it over his shoulder. "I'm about to go. You got this from here—" He readjusted his glasses. "Michael, is that you?"

Mr. Bryne smiled widely at him, tipping his drink toward Sal. "Still remember me?"

I furrowed my brows. "You guys know each other?"

Sal put a shaky hand on Mr. Bryne's shoulder. "He used to work for me. Almost thirty years ago."

"It's been that long, huh?"

"Best worker I ever had," Sal said, nudging me. "Besides you."

"She could learn a trick or two," Mr. Bryne said, winking at me with those devilish eyes.

"Well"—Sal squeezed Mr. Bryne's shoulder—"it was nice seeing you. Come in more often. Maybe Mia can show *you* how it's done."

Mr. Bryne nodded, and Sal turned toward the door.

"Do you need help?" I asked him, watching him struggle with his bag.

"Now, dear, don't you get me started. I'm still as agile as I used to be." He opened the door, then disappeared behind it. "See you tomorrow."

When the door closed and we were left in the empty bar, I turned back to Mr. Bryne to see him staring at me and … smiling. I stared back, heart pounding in my chest.

"What do you want?" I asked. "Why are you here?"

"I can't have a drink?"

"Why are you *still* here?" I said, rephrasing my question.

"Because I'm not finished." He tipped his very empty glass in my direction, and I arched a brow at him.

"Looks like you're finished to me."

I reached for his glass to put it away, but he grabbed my wrist instead, tingles erupting on it. I cursed myself for feeling this way, knowing that it'd break my heart in the end when he found out about Mom and started to treat me like everyone else who knew.

"How's Mason?" he asked, voice low.

"Sounds like you're jealous." The words tumbled out of my mouth before I could stop them, and I wished they hadn't.

Hell, he hadn't sounded jealous at all, but why else would he come to the place where he knew I worked and sit at the bar for hours until it was closing time, just to talk to me?

I had been coming up with explanations in my head all night, and jealousy was the only one that made sense.

"Oh, Mia," he said, chuckling.

He stood up and walked around the bar. I stared at his seat, heat warming my entire body.

"I'm not jealous over that boy. The only thing he has that I don't is you." He snaked a hand around my throat from behind and pulled me closer to him. "But I can have you in other ways."

His hand dipped between my legs, and I tried so damn hard to get myself to push it away ... but I couldn't.

"Mr. Bryne ... we can't."

I had said those words so many times before that they were starting to lose their meaning. But this time, I really meant them. I wasn't saying it because he was Melissa's dad. I was saying it because this was wrong. He placed his fingers against the front of my pants and rubbed my clit. So very, very wrong.

My fingers paled as I pressed them into the counter. *Mia, think of Mason. Think of all the good times you've spent with that boy ...*

But I couldn't remember any.

I brushed my fingers against his wrist, leaning back into his touch. "Mr. Bryne ..." I said softly.

"Say my name, Mia," he mumbled against my neck. He left a trail of sloppy, wet kisses all the way up my neck to my jaw. "I want to hear my name on your lips, want to hear you moaning it."

"The only way," I started, feeling his fingers slip into my panties, "you're going to hear me moaning your name"—his fingers played with my folds, spreading them apart and slipping between them—"is if you *make me* moan it."

He drew his fingers down my folds and against my entrance. He chuckled against my ear. "You either don't know how easy that is"—he rubbed his finger against my entrance, harder but never pushing it into me—"or you don't care."

I clenched and squeezed my eyes shut, wanting nothing more than for him to push his finger inside of me. He bit down on my neck, sucking the skin between his lips, almost enough to leave a hickey.

"Which is it?" He pressed his cock into my backside, grinding it more and more, and I curved my back, so I could feel him against my pussy.

He felt so big, so thick. And all I fucking wanted was for him to ram it into me.

I reached back to take it in my hand, but he snatched my wrist.

"Say it, Mia. Say my name, and I'll let you suck my cock."

My pussy tightened, heat warming my core. I gulped, my whole body aching for it. "Please ..." I whispered.

He rubbed his fingers around my clit, driving me higher and higher. I gripped on to the counter to steady my trembling legs. He was going to make me ... make me ...

He pulled his hand away just as I was about to come and pressed his cock flush against me.

My panties were soaked, my cunt pulsing. I needed his cock inside of it.

"Please," I begged Mr. Bryne. "I need it."

He pressed his fingers back against my clit, rubbing them faster than he had before. His hand tightened around my throat. I tightened yet again and whimpered, the pressure in my pussy rising with every second. And now ... now, I didn't want him to stop.

I parted my lips as I was about to come and said, "Michael, please don't stop."

Instead of pulling his hand away, he rubbed my swollen clit faster. My knees buckled, and I grasped on to the bar to hold myself up as I came for him.

He leaned over me, fingers pressing into the side of my neck, and smirked against my ear. "Say it again."

"Michael," I whispered, feeling nothing but ecstasy roll through me.

He groaned into my ear, pulled my shirt and bra cups down, and gazed at my tits from over my shoulder. He pulled both of my arms behind my back with one of his and thrust his cock against my ass again, watching my breasts bounce. "Fuck, Mia, these tits."

He pushed his hips into me. "Feel that?" he asked. "Beg for it like I know you want to." He took my nipple between his fingers and tugged on it, making me moan.

"Please, Michael ... please give it to me. I need it." My whole body was aching for it. I needed to feel full, needed his huge cock in my pussy, pounding in and out and making me moan for him.

"Louder." He squeezed my nipple, twisting it, then releasing it. Again and again.

I whimpered. "Please, Michael," I said louder. I reached behind me, drawing my hand up his cock through his pants. "Let me suck it."

He released my wrists, and I knelt behind the bar, rubbing my hand up and down his length. He undid his button and pulled down the zipper of his pants, pulling out his cock. I wrapped my hand around the base, licking from the base to his head while I stared up at him.

I swirled my tongue around his head, sucking on it gently. It was so big, and my pussy was throbbing, waiting for it to be inside of me.

"Fuck my mouth," I said to him, staring up at him with big eyes. "Please, Michael. Make me feel good."

His jaw twitched, his eyes full with lust. He grabbed my chin and pulled me toward him, pushing his cock into my mouth and teasing me with his head. "Touch yourself while I do it. Get your pussy ready for me to tear up," he said.

I pushed a hand between my legs and rubbed my clit through my underwear. He steadily pushed himself all the way into my throat until the base of his cock was against my lips. I roughly bobbed my head back and forth on him.

With one hand, Michael reached down and pinched my nipple between his fingers. A gush of pleasure rushed through me, and I tightened again. Drool dripped from my lips onto my breasts, and he rubbed the spit against my nipples, making them glisten.

He drove himself all the way down my throat, holding himself there. I stared up at him, cheeks warming, trying so desperately to breathe. I placed one hand on his thigh, trying to pull away, yet he held me close to him.

"Don't stop touching your pussy," he said, sliding deeper.

I squeezed my eyes closed, pushing him deeper down my throat and rubbing my pussy so fucking hard. It was pulsing more than it ever had.

My pussy tightened, and I moaned on Michael's cock. I could feel a toe-curling orgasm about to rip through me at any fucking moment.

Michael clutched my chin and made me look up at him. "Come."

And ... just like that ... I screamed out on his cock, delight rolling through me. He thrust his cock deeper, listening to the sloppy, wet gagging sounds my throat was making for him.

My legs tingled; my pussy pulsed. Before I even came down from the orgasm, he pulled me to my feet, turned me around to face the bar, and pushed my upper body down onto it. In one quick motion, he pulled my pants down to my ankles and pushed his cock right against my entrance, toying with me again.

"I've been thinking about this all fucking day," he said, plunging himself inside of me.

I arched my back and screamed out his name when he filled me. He lifted one of my legs, holding it in the air to give himself better access, and pounded into me.

"Harder, Michael," I said.

He snaked his arm around my waist, fingers rubbing my clit.

I tightened my grip on the bar, my pussy tensing. And I didn't know what possessed me to say what I said next, but ... God ... it had to be the fucking devil. "Please come inside of me," I said, my mind hazy. "Please, I need it."

He groaned into my ear, body shuddering, and bit down on

my neck. Rapture exploded through me, and I furrowed my brows.

"God, Michael, I can't fucking handle it anymore. I-I'm ... I'm going to—"

"Come. I want to feel your pussy tighten around me," he said.

The tension built high inside me. I gripped on to the counter, trying to hold on to something as my pussy quivered over and over and over on his cock.

"Let me come on your tits," he said against me, breathing hitched.

I clenched on him, and he tensed.

"Mia, please."

Yet he didn't stop pounding into me. My cunt filled with warmth, nipples rubbing against the bar.

"Mia ..."

I slid down to my knees, crossed my arms under my breasts to hold them together, and looked up at him through my lashes. He jerked his cock, lips parted and eyes fixed on me.

"Why don't you come on my face instead?" I asked.

He placed a hand on my chin, holding me steady, and came all over my lips. He groaned quietly to himself, closing his eyes, and I stood up and swept the cum off the corner of my lips with my finger. He stumbled back and took a deep breath, gazing at me with those sinister eyes again. Those eyes that made me feel things I shouldn't.

I grabbed my clothes and a glass of water from the sink, listening to my phone buzz on the counter. *Orangegate Assisted Living* flashed on my screen. *Mom? Why is she calling this late?* Usually, when she called, it was on her own phone.

"Hello?" I said, picking up a glass of water and gulping it down. After *that*, I needed to cool down before I talked to her.

"Mia?" Susan said through the phone, her voice laced with worry.

I furrowed my brows. "Yes? Is everything okay?"

"Your mother …"

My heart dropped. "What about Mom?"

"Your mother had another brain aneurysm."

The glass fell from my hand. The sound of it shattering against the counter echoed throughout the room. My heart dropped.

Mom had another brain aneurysm? Another one? I gulped.

"No," I whispered. No. I'd just seen her. Everything was okay. Everything had been fine. "You—you're lying. Tell me you're lying."

"She's at the hospital now."

Oh my God. What had she done to deserve this? She'd worked so hard to get better. So damn hard. And now … this …

My lips trembled. She wouldn't recover from this one. It was a miracle she'd recovered from the first. A second one would kill her.

CHAPTER 16

MIA

"Mia," Michael said, brows furrowed together.

He stared at me with eyes filled with pure worry, and ... and it felt weird. He hadn't looked at me like that before. No man had looked at me like that for years.

The phone fell from my hand, and my upper body collapsed onto the bar counter, a shrill cry escaping my lips. No, this couldn't be happening again. This ... I ...

My eyes filled with tears, and I didn't even try to stop them from rushing down my face.

I could distantly hear Susan talking through the phone that was now on the ground, and I stomped right on it to shut her up. If I hadn't left Mom there ... if I had brought her home with me, maybe it wouldn't have happened. Maybe—another loud cry—maybe she still would have been happy and healthy.

Michael pulled my upper body off the counter, trying to hold me upright. "Shit ..." he said under his breath.

I gazed down at the counter to see broken glass, spilled water, and blood—my blood.

"We have to get you cleaned up."

He steered me toward the restroom, but I pulled away from him.

"No, I have to go." I hurried toward the door, not even feeling any pain from the glass still deep in my arms.

"You're not going anywhere," he said, carefully snatching my wrist. "Not until the glass is out of your arms."

My lips quivered, and I turned around to face him. "No …" I shook my head. "I have to go. You don't understand. Mom is going to die." Tears streamed down my face. "She's going to die, and I can't do anything about it."

I thought I could tell that he didn't know what to say. But then he took my hand in his, squeezed tightly, and brought me toward the restroom.

"Give me two minutes. Then, I'll take you wherever you need to go."

I let him because the glass would have to come out sooner or later, and Mom would be disappointed if she found out I'd rushed to the hospital—when she still had to be in surgery—with glass in my arms and blood gushing out of my wounds.

"Please, be quick."

After pushing open the restroom door, he turned on the sink, lifted my arm, and looked into my eyes. "This might hurt." He carefully took a piece of glass between his fingers and started to pull.

Pain shot up my arm, and I seized his bicep, my fingers curling into it. "Michael …" I said. "Just pull."

He hesitated, then pulled it out of my arm, immediately covering my wound with a bunch of paper towels. He threw the piece in the garbage and started on the second one, which hurt even worse. I rested my head against his shoulder, trying to take deep breaths to disperse the pain ... but the hurt festered inside of me.

And I honestly couldn't tell the difference between the physical pain of my cuts and the pain of hearing that Mom was close to death. She was my rock, the only thing that kept me happy in this shitty life I had to endure.

More tears streamed down my cheeks, and my body heaved back and forth. I didn't want to lose her. I couldn't lose her. All of this would have been for nothing. My life would be meaningless without her in it.

"Stay here," Michael said, disappearing into the hallway. "I'm going to get some bandages."

"The first-aid kit is—"

"I know," he said, walking back into the room with the first-aid kit. The corners of his lips were turned up in an attempt to make light of the conversation. "I haven't forgotten." He washed the blood off my arms and wrapped some gauze around them.

I stared at him while he helped me, frowning. He glanced down at me, spinning the gauze around my arm, his gray eyes so soft that I felt ... I felt safe. And again, that feeling was so unfamiliar it made me shiver in fear. Yet part of me wanted more of it. I wanted to feel safe and cared for like *this* all the time. Not only when it mattered.

When he finished, I wiped my tears with the back of my hand and hurried out of the bathroom, desperate to get to Mom as soon as I could. I grabbed my bag and locked the bar doors, spotting Michael's car.

I started toward it, then stopped. If I let him take me, he would find out about Mom and how this had happened before. He'd start to look at me differently. He'd pity me for what had happened to my family.

"Mia," he said, nodding toward his car, "let's go."

But ... taking the bus would add another hour that I didn't have. I swallowed my pride and walked with him toward his car, sliding into the passenger seat and gripping my bag as if it held my entire life in it.

"Can you drive me to Mercy Hospital?"

Within ten minutes, we were standing at the reception desk at Mercy, waiting for the fucking woman to get off the phone. She looked up at me through her lashes, giving me that *please wait* stare.

She hung up the phone, smiled sweetly at me—as if she hadn't just scolded me with her eyes—and asked, "How can I help you?"

"My mother. Eden Stevenson. Where is she?"

She typed something into her computer and frowned. "Eden Stevenson is being moved to the ICU as we speak. Go down the hall—"

Before she could finish, I hurried down the hallway. I had been here about a thousand times before; I knew where it was. Michael stepped onto the elevator with me, and I pressed the button for the fourth floor a million times.

If Mom was in the ICU, that meant she had made it out of surgery already. But being out of her first surgery didn't mean that this was all over. She would go through more, the hospital bills would pile even higher, and soon, even Mason wouldn't want to help me with her.

When I made it to the fourth floor, I hurried to the front desk. "Eden Stevenson?"

The woman, much friendlier than the other one, smiled at me. "She's still being moved up here. Once we get her settled in, I will let you know. For now, you can wait in the waiting room."

Michael placed his hand on my upper back, guiding me to the waiting room. I sat next to him, my knees bouncing, and dialed Mason's number. The call went to voice mail, so I hung up and called him again.

When he didn't answer for a second time, I left him a message, my words coming out so fast that they sounded slurred. "Mason, please, pick up the phone. My mom is back in the ICU."

After I hung up, I pursed my lips and texted Melissa and Serena.

Me: Please meet me at Mercy.

My frown deepened when I didn't receive an immediate response back, and I sank into the chair.

Michael looked over at me, his knee grazing against mine. "What do you mean, your mother is *back* here? She's been here before?"

My heart ached, and I gazed into his gray eyes. This was it. This was when he'd start treating me differently. Things wouldn't ever be the same from now on.

I nodded and wrapped my arms around my body. "About four years ago, she had a brain aneurysm. She's been stuck in assisted living"—I shook my head, hoping more tears wouldn't fall—"when she should've been living with me."

"Mia," he said, voice gentle, "I didn't know. Why didn't you tell me?"

I stared down at my knees and didn't say a word. I was ashamed, so ashamed that I couldn't support myself and that I had to use Mason for money.

When I didn't say anything, he sighed through his nose. And then he placed a hesitant hand on my knee and squeezed lightly, fingers brushing against the inside of my thigh. It was unlike any other time he had touched me. His touch was so gentle.

"What about your father? Should you call him?"

And that was when I burst into tears.

"My dad …" I whispered. My body heaved back and forth, and I tried so hard to hold myself still, but I couldn't. I hung my head in shame—more damn shame. It was all I felt.

By the way Michael shifted beside me, I could tell that he wanted to comfort me more than he already was, but he was hesitant. "Mia, you don't have to tell me."

"My dad hit my mom, cheated on her, took all her damn money, and left us." It was the first time I had ever said those words out loud. I hadn't dared say them before to Mason—he already knew what had happened. I didn't dare say them to Melissa and Serena—I didn't want them to know. I hadn't even said the words to myself because that would make it so much more real than it already was.

All I could feel was pain from it because ... I was turning into my father without even trying to. I was taking Mason's money. I was mooching off of him. I was cheating on him with Michael. And I might've felt guilty about the money part, but I didn't feel guilty about—I gazed down at Michael's hand resting on my knee—this part.

Michael looked down and clenched his jaw.

I didn't know how long we sat in silence, but it had to have been almost an hour. The nurse hadn't called us up to the counter, and I was getting anxious. Michael's hand hadn't left my knee, only calming me down for a bit.

CHAPTER 17

MIA

The elevator doors opened, and Mason walked out of the elevator with Melissa and Serena. I hopped up from my chair, so Mason didn't see Michael's hand on my knee and hurried over to him.

A look of worry crossed his face for a brief moment, and he wrapped his arms around me. "Baby, what's going on?" he asked, pulling away from me.

"Mom had another brain aneurysm," I whispered.

He looked down at my bandaged arms, then back up at me. "And these?"

I pulled my arms away from him and shook my head. "I got cut with glass at work."

Then, after those two simple questions, he gazed over at Michael. "You called Melissa's dad to come here before me?"

I pressed my lips together, heart pounding in my chest. Why was he jealous at a time like this? Why was he constantly jealous? Up until recently, I had done nothing to him. I was his perfect girlfriend; I let him go out with the guys, sacrificed nights out with the girls, didn't talk to any other man that he didn't want me to. And he was jealous while my mom was being transported into intensive care.

"I didn't call him," I said through gritted teeth. "He was at the bar when I got the call." I pulled away from him and walked to the other side of the waiting room, sat in a chair, and stared at the ground.

If I wanted to get out of this relationship with Mason, I couldn't ask him to help me with these bills; I'd be in his debt forever. I had to either do it myself or …

I took a deep breath and pulled out my phone. Scrolling through my Contacts, my thumb hovered over *his* name.

After a few moments, I put the phone back into my pocket. No, I couldn't do that. He didn't care about Mom and me. He wouldn't have left us if he did. I couldn't call Dad, not even if Mom survived. But … I wasn't sure I had a choice.

Dr. Jackson—the same doctor Mom had had last time—walked out into the waiting room, stuffing a pen into his pocket. "Family of Eden Stevenson?"

I shot up from my chair. "Is she okay? Is she stable? Can I see her?"

The doctor smiled at me and nodded. "Nice to see you again, Mia," he said. He paused and gulped. "Your mother is in stable condition *for now*. She has a couple more surgeries scheduled for later on this week. But as I told you last time, it was a miracle she recovered so quickly. Many people don't." He took a deep breath. "There is a high likelihood that, if she survives, she won't ever get back to fully functioning like she was again."

Tears rolled down my cheeks, and I nodded. I had known it. I had known that this was what he'd tell me, but hearing it … felt worse than I'd expected.

What was I going to do? How could I help Mom when I couldn't even help myself?

"Can I see her?" I asked.

"She's not conscious now, but you're welcome to check in on her." He glanced around the room, noticing the four others with me. "But only one at a time, please."

I followed him through the hallways and glanced into the room she had been in last time—room 405. The numbers had haunted my dreams too much these past few years. He nodded toward room 418, and I hesitantly stepped into the room.

Mom lay in the bed, her head shaved to the skin, more scars on her scalp. There was a feeding tube in her neck and an oxygen tube in her nose. More tears welled up in my eyes.

I grabbed her hand and intertwined our fingers. "Mom," I whispered, knowing she couldn't hear me. "Mom, it's going to be okay. I promise you that I'm going to do everything I can to get you better."

And I would do anything I had to do to get her healthier again. I would quit school. I would quit my job. I would dump Mason and find us a studio apartment down in the slums, if I had to. Anything to spend more time with her like we used to.

When the doctor ushered me out, I gave her one last kiss and walked toward the door. And then I closed my eyes, stepped out into the hallway, and dialed Dad's number. I couldn't afford any more hospital bills, and I didn't want us to be in debt forever. The phone rang and rang and rang, and as I was about to hang up, he answered.

"Mia," he said in a gruff voice. "Didn't think I'd ever hear from you again."

My lips quivered at the mere sound of his voice. I wanted to hang up the phone right then and there. Even though all I had for him was anger, I couldn't hang up. "Dad."

He chuckled so menacingly at me. "Didn't think I'd ever hear that again either."

"Mom's in the hospital again."

All his pleasantries went right out the window, and the real him finally showed up. "Why are you calling me? Do you think I give a fuck about your mother? She was nothing but a nag."

Tears welled up in my eyes, and I tried to keep my voice quiet, so nobody would hear that I needed help with my finances. It was embarrassing, to say the least. "Dad, please … I can't afford any more hospital bills. We already lost the house."

I felt so shitty for calling him. I had known he wouldn't help me.

"You're the only person I have who can help me," I whispered, brushing a stray tear off my cheek. Some nurses walked down the hall, and I leaned against the wall, resting my forehead on it. "Please."

"No."

"What do you want me to do?" I asked desperately. "I'll do anything. All I need is a few thousand." It was a lie. I needed more. Way more. But anything would do right now.

"No," he said again, his voice stern. "Your mother is not my problem anymore."

"What about me?" I asked, louder than I'd meant to. "I'm your daughter." I turned around. When I saw Mason look into the hallway from the waiting room, I quieted my voice. "I'm your daughter, and I'm struggling. Don't you care about me?"

He stayed silent for a long time, then sighed through his nose. "You're an adult, Mia."

"And you're an asshole," I said, slamming my already-cracked phone on the ground, shoving my back against the wall, and sliding down it. "Just a fucking asshole."

CHAPTER 18

MIA

Two weeks had gone by since Mom was taken into the hospital. Because they hadn't let me sleep in Mom's room, I slept in the waiting room every night, even when the nurses said that visiting hours were over. Mom had been through a dozen surgeries and survived each one. But I wanted to be here in case anything happened.

I told Sal what had happened, and he gave me the entire month off, but he expected me back soon. I knew that he wouldn't be able to keep my job open for me forever.

In the hallway, I stared through the glass window into Mom's room, watching her open her eyes and look up at the doctor. She only moved a couple inches to readjust her head, but it was something. And I was happy about it.

"Everything with Orangegate Assisted Living is dealt with," Mason said, standing next to me in the hallway.

Mason had stopped making payments to Orangegate Assisted Living after I told him Mom wasn't going back there—ever.

He squeezed my shoulder and leaned into me. "I gotta go. Are you sure you don't want to come home tonight?"

After nodding my head, I watched him disappear down the hallway and head toward the waiting room. He didn't have to say anything for me to be able to tell that this was taking a toll on him. He had dealt with my family shit once already, and now, he had to deal with it a second time.

"How is she?" Michael asked, walking up behind me.

Still in his suit for work, he stood beside me with his briefcase hanging off his shoulder and takeout in his hand. I glanced up at him.

This hospital was taking a toll on me too.

With his lips pulled into a smile, he lifted the takeout bag. "Italian grinders. Mayo, oil, lettuce, and tomato." He handed me the bag. "And I didn't forget to ask for a side of chips this time."

My heart grew warm, and I glanced from him to Mom. She lifted her hand a few inches off the bed and curled her fingers at Michael to say hello. He waved back at her and smiled. She lay back down and closed her eyes, taking a deep breath.

"Are you staying?" I asked, hoping that he didn't have to leave early like he had last night because this stress was getting to me … and I needed something to help me relax. And by something, I meant him. I glanced down at his lips, watching his tongue glide over his teeth and feeling the heat gather inside of me.

"Yes." He stared down at me with those playful eyes, took the bag from me, grabbed my hand, and placed the bag in the corner of the waiting room that I had completely taken over. "This can wait."

I sucked in a deep breath, every part of my body starting to warm. Michael glanced down the hallway, pulled me toward a door, and slipped me into the supply closet. He closed the door behind us, pinned me against it, and kissed me.

Two long fucking weeks without this.

My fingers plunged into his hair, and I tugged on it to pull him closer. He ground his stiffness against my stomach, making me tighten, and left a trail of sloppy, wet kisses down the column of my neck, nibbling on the skin.

I moaned and pushed my hand against the front of his pants, stroking his cock through them. "Please, give it to me, Michael. God, I've been waiting for this for weeks."

He slid his hands under my shirt, unclipped my bra, and groped my breasts. I moaned, my nipples taut against his palms.

"Mia …" he said, groaning against my ear as he pushed his bulge harder against my hand. "Everything about you …"

While I wanted to hear what he had to say about me, I couldn't wait one more moment. I hungrily pressed my lips to his, and then I turned around, pulled down my leggings, posted my hands against the door, and stared back at him. "Make it rough."

His gaze traveled from my eyes, all the way down my back, to my ass. He undid his belt and zipper, and then he pulled out his cock and harshly pushed me against the door. After gently pushing the side of my face flat against it, he rubbed his cock against my ass.

"Spread your legs." He smacked the insides of my thighs with his palm.

I spread my legs apart and waited for him to thrust into me. The head of his cock rubbed against my wetness, and my pussy pulsed.

He continued to rub it against my pussy, not entering me, and then slapped it roughly against my clit, making me moan. A surge of pleasure rushed through my body. He slapped my pussy again and again with his cock. I squeezed my legs together, unable to contain the ecstasy coursing through me. I needed a release more than I needed anything right now.

"Please, Michael."

Michael shoved his cock against my folds, grabbed a fistful of my hair, and pulled me against him. "I said, spread your fucking legs, Mia. Don't make me say it again."

I spread my legs wider for him, my pussy pulsing, waiting for him to take me. "Please."

"Please what?" he mumbled against my ear.

"Please, fuck me hard."

He slapped his cock on my pussy again, and I moaned. The tension rose in my core, pushing me closer and closer to the edge of coming already, and he hadn't even put it inside of me yet.

He smirked against my neck and lightly sank his teeth into my shoulder, and then he rammed himself deep inside of me. I screamed out in delight. He drove into me with one hand wrapped in my hair.

"Harder."

He slipped his other hand around my waist to my tits, and he slapped one tit through my shirt and watched it bounce.

"More."

He struck my breast again with his palm, hitting my nipple. I moaned out, the force building inside my pussy. The hand that was tangled in my hair wrapped around the front of my throat, and he squeezed lightly.

"Harder," I choked out. "Please."

He growled against my ear, pushed his hand down to my clit, and smacked it over and over and over until it was swollen under his fingers. Every time he hit me—every fucking time—I clenched tighter and tighter on his cock. He slammed into me, and I gripped his wrist as the lust pulsed throughout my body.

"Don't stop fucking me, Michael …" I breathed out. "Don't stop fucking me until you come."

He started to pump even faster inside of me, fingers rubbing my clit. I drew my fingers over my nipple, threw my head back, and squeezed my eyes closed. So close … so damn close. So many emotions were pumping through me that I didn't even realize that Michael had loosened his grip on my neck and pressed his lips to mine.

"Mia," he mumbled, "I'm going to come inside of you."

As soon as the words left his mouth, I came all over his cock. My pussy was pulsing, my legs shaking, my mind numb. He dug his fingers lightly into my hips, shoved his cock as deep as it would go, and stilled.

I relaxed against him, my eyes rolling back into my head. He started to pull out of me, and I could feel my pussy gripping on to every inch of his cock.

After a few moments, I reclipped my bra, pulled up my pants, and took a deep breath. My legs were still tingling, my whole body relaxing for the slightest moment. I gathered all my thoughts and peeked my head out the door, making sure the coast was clear. When I was sure that it was, Michael and I walked out of the room.

"Mia?" someone said from behind me.

I turned around to see Serena, staring wide-eyed at me and *Melissa's father* coming out of the supply closet together.

CHAPTER 19

MIA

Oh my fucking God.
 This couldn't be happening. I refused to believe it. *How can ...*

Serena gazed between us, lips parting, not uttering a single word. I stared at her and clasped my hands together, my heart pounding against my chest.

What should I say? Should I tell her? Should I act like nothing happened? Will she tell Melissa that I am sleeping with her father?

"Are you hungry, Serena?" Michael asked, trying to shake away the sudden tension.

But it didn't go away. I could feel the tension in the air, could already hear all the questions she was going to ask me about this.

Serena glanced at him, then down at her shoes. "Um, I don't want to intrude."

"You're not intruding," I said a bit too quickly. *Nice going, Mia. Way to look extra suspicious.* "Mich—" I pursed my lips, accidentally slipping his real name into the conversation, and cursed myself. "Mr. Bryne was just … leaving."

I didn't want Michael to leave. Besides spending time with Mom, I looked forward to eating dinner with him every night. It wasn't like anyone else came to visit me regularly here.

Michael nodded. "I'll, um … see you tomorrow night, Mia."

Though he tried to brush this off as if it were nothing, I could see that look in his eyes. He was nervous about being caught, almost as much as I was. But the Mr. Bryne I knew usually was never nervous. We'd fucked in his house with his daughter home, in the living room, in front of the damn window.

After sending me a strained smile, he disappeared into the elevator. I stared at the ground and walked toward the waiting room. Serena followed me in an uncomfortable silence. I took the sandwiches out of the takeout bag and handed mine to her, knowing that she wouldn't like the peppers on Michael's.

"So …" she said after we finished eating.

I opened the bag of chips and loudly crunched on one. Damn, this was way more awkward than I'd thought it would be.

"You and Melissa's dad? What was that about?"

For the first time tonight, I looked her right in her eyes and gulped. "Please don't tell Melissa. Please. Please. Please. I didn't mean for it to happen." Lie. "It just kind of did. I thought it was going to be a one-time thing."

Her eyes widened, and then there was a sudden playfulness in them. "This happened before?" She slapped me on the arm. "And you didn't tell me about it?"

My eyes widened, and I placed the chips on the table between us. *She is okay with it?*

"Girl! Remember we used to have the biggest crush on him in high school? We used to talk about what he'd be like in bed all the time behind Melissa's back. Did you forget or something?"

I sighed in relief. High school seemed like it was so long ago.

With all the shit that had happened since I graduated ... I barely remembered.

Serena inched closer to me. "So, tell me all the deets. I won't tell Melissa or Mason."

"Mason ..." I said, guilt plaguing me again.

She rolled her eyes. "Mia, don't even feel bad about him. It's about damn time you moved on from that lazy-ass man-whore. I usually don't condone cheating, but Mason doesn't do anything to please you. You complain about him all the time." She bumped her shoulder into mine. "So ... details. Now."

So, I grabbed my bag of chips and told her everything—from the night we'd first started hooking up to the summer party to him fucking me senseless at the bar. Her eyes were wide with excitement the whole time, and she was bouncing in her seat.

"God ..." She fanned herself. "You are living the freaking dream! Sleeping with our best friend's dad." She slumped down in her seat with the biggest smile on her face. "You don't know how excited I am to hear about all these little sexcapades. I am living for this."

I smiled and told her all about the night at the pool, but the elevator doors opened.

Melissa walked out of it, her hair messy and her face glowing, as if Victor had just given it to her good. "Hey, girls!"

She plopped down next to me and grabbed my hand. "I thought I'd come visit you. Mason said you were more stressed than usual today." She intertwined her fingers with mine. "So, I thought that I would get us into the hottest party of the summer to help you relax!"

I furrowed my brows at her. "What're you talking about?"

"Alpha Epsilon Pi," Melissa said, giving me a quizzical look. "Remember we went to one of their parties last year? It was the best college party I'd ever been to."

I sighed through my nose. "Melissa, I can't go to a party now. Mom is in the hospital."

What is she thinking? I couldn't leave.

She tilted her head in my direction. "Come on, Mia. You've been cooped up here for weeks, and you haven't left once. You need to get out for a couple hours, for your mental health."

My gaze shifted from her to Serena, who shrugged her shoulders. "You don't have to go for long. We can stay for a couple hours," she said. "It will be good for you, Mia."

"I bet Mama Eden wouldn't mind you getting out." Melissa winked at me.

I glanced back down the hallway toward Mom's room and stood up. "If she has a surgery scheduled for Friday or Saturday morning, I'm not going." I hurried toward her room and peeked my head into it. "Hey, Mom."

She opened her eyes and smiled softly. "Hi, hon. How is Mr. Bryne?"

After I closed the door behind me, I tensed. "Mr. Bryne is fine."

"He's been spending a lot of time here."

I scratched the back of my head. "Yeah ... he has," I said.

She paused for a long time, and I didn't know if she was waiting for me to continue, if she already knew about us, or if she needed more rest.

So, I said, "Do you need me to come back later?"

She shook her head. "No." She looked at the chair next to her. "Come and sit. You look stressed. Have you been eating? Drinking enough water? Sleeping well at home?"

"I told you that I'm not leaving the hospital until you can leave this place."

"You've been here this whole time?" she asked, brows furrowing together. "Darling, you have to go out. Get some fresh air. Goodness, you're probably more stressed than I am."

"Are you sure?" I asked, grasping her hand. "Melissa wants me to go to a party with her for only a couple hours on Friday night.

I won't be gone for long, but if you want me to stay, I will stay. I don't mind—"

"Go," Mom said. "Please. It will make me feel better that you're still getting out."

CHAPTER 20

MIA

It was Thursday night. All I wanted was to relax before the party tomorrow, and Michael showed up at the best time with the usual takeout. Dressed in that damn nice suit that fit him perfectly, his sleeves rolled up his muscular forearms, and my pussy was growing warmer by the damn second.

He sat down next to me in the hospital waiting room and placed the food down on the table in front of us. His brows were furrowed together, as if he had been stressed the entire day or was worried about something.

Before he could take out the sandwiches, I placed my hand on his knee and slid it up his thigh, aching for a release.

"Mia," he said sternly, his voice turning me on more. "Remember the last time we did this in public."

"The *Mr. Bryne* I know doesn't care about being caught," I said, smiling sweetly at him.

The tension in his face disappeared for a moment, and he shifted in his seat, placing his hand on my knee, then trailing it up my thigh. He slid his hand over my leggings and dipped them between my legs, rubbing my pussy through the thin material. I snatched the takeout bag from him and placed it over my legs, so if anyone walked by, they wouldn't be able to see him touching my pussy.

"Have you been thinking about this all day, Mia?"

I nodded and stared at him, watching his eyes grow playful. "More," I whispered.

"So desperate," he said, the corner of his lips curling up. He slipped his hand into my pants, hooked a finger inside my underwear, and pulled them to the side to rub small circles against my clit.

I blew out a shaky breath from my nose and balled the takeout bag in my fist. The pressure rose in my core, and I squeezed my knees together. God, I wished everyday could be like this with him.

"Keep your legs spread," he said, eyes hardening.

I clenched, heat exploding between my thighs, and spread my legs a bit more for him.

"More."

When I only spread them a few more inches, he grabbed my knee with his other hand and pulled it toward him, forcing me to spread my legs wide.

Then, he brushed his fingers up my thigh, up my abdomen, to my breast, and played with my nipple poking out of my shirt. "You were ready for me to come see you today," he said with that devilish smirk on his face.

His fingers quickened, and I could feel the tension building up inside me. I dug my nails into him, unable to hold off my orgasm much longer.

A family walked into the waiting room, yet Michael didn't stop. He dragged his fingertip across my nipple—back and forth, back and forth—making me tighten. I scooted in my seat, hoping that the family wouldn't notice.

And then he pushed his fingers into me, starting to pump them in and out. "Are you going to moan for me, Mia?" he asked in my ear. "Or am I going to have to make you again?"

I could hear his finger thrusting into my wetness. He moved his fingers faster, and I shut my eyes tightly.

"Michael," I whispered, holding his wrist even tighter. The force drove me higher and higher by the damn second.

"Your pussy feels so tight around my fingers," he said. "I want to feel you tightening around *this*." He grabbed my hand and placed it on the bulge in his pants. Right out in the damn open, like he didn't care who saw.

I bit my lip, hoping to not make a sound. He groped my breast again, and I took another shaky breath.

God help me.

When he curled his fingers inside me, immediately hitting my G-spot, he slapped a hand over my mouth to muffle my moan. "Shh, shh, shh."

My pussy was pulsing on him, my legs trembling. Wave after wave of pleasure shot through me.

After a few moments, he pulled his fingers out of my pussy, stuck them into his mouth, and relaxed beside me. And then, as if nothing had happened, he wiped them on a napkin, and we ate our dinner in silence.

"I want to talk to you," Michael said, balling up his sandwich wrapper and throwing it into the bag.

I swallowed my food and sat up, grazing my knee against his.

There was a lot I wanted to *talk* about with him because though I had just orgasmed, I was greedy. I wanted more. I wanted *him*. For a split second, his gaze drifted from my legs to my hips, then back to my face, and he reluctantly restrained himself.

"Not that."

My lips formed an O, and I tossed my wrapper into the brown paper bag with his, wiping my fingers on a napkin. A hundred things raced through my mind about what it could be. My stomach turned, and I felt like he was about to say something really, really bad. He hadn't treated me any differently since Mom had come to the hospital, but ... I had been waiting for this *talk* for a couple weeks now.

"What do you want to talk about?" I asked, gnawing on the inside of my cheek.

He rubbed his face and broke eye contact with me. "I've been thinking about this for a while. I haven't known how to say it."

My stomach tightened, and I gulped. *Here it comes ...*

"I heard the conversation you had with your father a couple weeks ago."

Fuck.

My cheeks flushed. He'd heard how desperate I was for money. He knew how much I needed it and how ... how I couldn't support myself. I parted my lips to say something, but nothing would come out.

It didn't seem like he knew what to say either because he didn't say anything for the longest time.

And then he said what I feared the most. "How much do you need?"

All I felt was shame and guilt and so many emotions that I hadn't even known I had.

I shook my head and looked him right in the eye. "I don't need anything."

I didn't want his money or that pitiful look he was giving me.

"Mia," he said, carefully choosing his next words. "Don't be difficult. All I want to do is help you. There's nothing wrong with accepting money from someone else."

My heart pounded in my chest, and something inside of me snapped. "If you want to help me out, you'll stop talking about this right now and go fuck me in the damn supply closet," I said, gaze rigid. "Because I don't want your money or sorrow or even compassion. I just want sex."

As soon as the words left my mouth, I wished they hadn't. I hadn't meant for it to come out so harsh and so ... so cruel. It sounded like I didn't have any feelings for him at all ... when I did. There was more to us than late-night encounters and sneaking into storage closets. Hell, I *wanted* more than this. But ... it couldn't happen. It was bad enough we were hooking up. We'd never be able to have a real relationship.

An unreadable expression crossed his face, and then he tightened his jaw. "You're either lying to yourself or you're blind, Mia," he said. "You deserve more than what Mason has been giving you."

"Oh, so *he* is what you really want to talk about," I said. And again, I couldn't seem to stop myself.

I didn't want to feel like a pitiful mess. I didn't want to feel like I owed Michael. I wanted to keep our relationship the way it was ...

Because I was scared.

Michael's eyes hardened. "He hasn't come to visit you all week, and when he does, he flirts with all the nurses at the front desk."

My heart ached, and I grasped on to the seat, knuckles turning white. "I know what he does," I snapped. "You don't have to make me feel worse about it."

Michael stood up and ran his hands through his hair. "I don't understand you, Mia." He sighed and shook his head at me. "I don't understand why you deal with his shit. He doesn't give a fuck about you, and you let him walk all over you. But when someone does care, when someone wants to help you out of this situation ... all you want from them is sex?"

I gulped and stared at him. *No, that's not all I want.* I wanted to scream those words at him, wanted him to hold me ... but I didn't want to screw things up with him. I had screwed things up with every guy in my life, except Michael. And I didn't want to ruin the relationship we already had.

After gathering all my damn strength—knowing that one way or another, we wouldn't last—I looked him right in the eye. Might as well stop this little game now before things got serious between us.

"I don't want anything more," I lied, my eyes becoming glossy. "All I ever wanted from you was sex."

He stared at me with so much hurt, waiting for me to take it back, waiting for me to break down into tears, but I refused to. I would suffer more now, so I wouldn't suffer later.

His gaze dropped to the ground, and he shook his head, jaw clenched. "Fine." He grabbed his suit jacket and slung it over his shoulder. "Then, I should go."

And then he walked to the elevator, not sparing me another glance.

CHAPTER 21

MIA

When the elevator doors had closed last night, I'd felt nothing but pain and regret. I'd wanted to run down the stairs, meet him on the ground floor, tell him that I didn't mean any of it, that I was just hurting really badly ... but I couldn't get myself to move from my spot.

I glanced into the hospital bathroom mirror, promised myself that I wouldn't cry again, and applied some mascara. The light in this room wasn't the best for putting on makeup, but I didn't have a way to get home to get ready there.

The bathroom door opened, and I listened to someone sigh.

"Mia, are you seriously getting ready in the damn hospital?" Serena asked. She walked over to me and grabbed the mascara, tilted my head toward her, and started applying it for me. "Let me help."

After taking a deep breath, I let myself relax. At least I hadn't pushed Serena or Melissa away yet. They were the only people who could support me through this now.

"So," she said, smiling, "how are you and *Michael*?"

I frowned, tears welling up in my eyes. *Don't cry, Mia. You're the one who pushed him away.* "I'd rather not talk about him," I said.

She furrowed her brows. "But you were—"

"What's taking you girls so long?" Melissa asked, popping her head into the bathroom. "The guys are waiting for us at the party already. It started ten minutes ago." She walked into the bathroom, saw Serena doing my makeup, and pulled a stick of red lipstick out of her purse. "Here, try this." She grabbed my chin and applied a coat on my lips. "Perfect!"

I snuck Serena a glance, wanting to continue the conversation with someone because it was driving me insane. I wanted her to tell me that I had made the right choice, that telling Michael all I wanted from him was sex was what I was supposed to do, because I couldn't tell Melissa. I couldn't mention it to her. I couldn't even tell her that I was seeing someone on the side.

She'd pry.

She'd ask everyone who it was.

She'd find out that it was her own father.

During the whole drive to the party, I sat in the backseat with my knees bouncing wildly. I shouldn't have left Mom. I should've stayed at the hospital, had a lonely night to myself, and thought about how I ruined every single relationship I ever had. How I was a fucking monster who couldn't stop hurting people or hurting myself.

When we pulled up to *the biggest party of the summer*, I sighed quietly through my nose. I'd only stay for a couple hours, and then I'd have Melissa bring me to see Mom. And if Melissa was too preoccupied with Victor, then I'd ask Mason.

There were over twenty cars parked on the street, and people were walking toward the house in droves. Lights were flashing from inside, a heap of smoke was drifting out from the front door, and music was blaring through the damn windows.

Melissa took my hand and pulled me into the house with her.

Serena disappeared into the crowd as soon as she saw her boyfriend. I stood by Melissa's side for what seemed like hours before Serena told me she was leaving early because her boyfriend's sister was in labor.

It wasn't even ten yet, and I wanted to ask Serena to take me back to the hospital, but she was in too much of a rush to hear a word I said—I didn't blame her, though. She didn't need all my drama right now.

I slumped down on a chair, watching people strip almost naked by the pool and start freaking skinny-dipping as a group of frat boys cheered them on. Melissa stumbled up to me with a beer in her hand.

I gazed up at her through my lashes. "I want to go home."

Melissa grabbed my hand and pulled me off the chair and back into the house. "Oh, come on, Mia!" she said, slurring her words.

I could smell the stench of alcohol on her breath, coming off in damn waves.

I scrunched my nose. "Melissa, please …" I said, but then shut my mouth.

Neither she nor Mason could drive me home. They were both already too drunk to even think straight.

She continued to push people out of the way until we reached the stairs. The dreaded damn stairs where couples were walking up—about to go fuck in a random person's bedroom, where people didn't give two fucks about STDs, cheating, or if the other person was wearing a condom.

When she started to pull me upstairs, I tugged my hand away from her. "Melissa, what're you doing?"

She clutched on to the railing for support and grabbed my hand again. "Please, come up here with me. I have a surprise for you."

"Is it someone who is sober who can drive me home?"

With glossy eyes, she looked up the stairs. "No," she said with a drunken smile plastered on her face. She tugged on my wrist and literally almost dragged me up the damn stairs with her. "It's something better."

Again, I pulled my hand away from her. "No, we need to—"

A frat boy walked down the stairs, looking Melissa up and down with a lustful grin on his face. "Looking good, Melissa," he said, hand brushing against her waist. "You wanna come down by the pool with us?" His eyebrows moved up and down suggestively.

Melissa looked at me, then at the pool, as if she was actually thinking about getting naked in front of everyone. I cursed under my breath and ushered her up the stairs.

"No," I said to whatever the fuck his name was. "We're busy."

Once we made it to the second floor, I sighed and closed my eyes. This was why I didn't go to stupid fucking parties anymore. All these damn frat boys, wanting to see everyone at the fucking party naked, deciding who they got to sleep with that night—not caring if the girl they chose had a boyfriend and not caring if that girl was sober enough to actually consent.

It was disgusting. Absolutely disgusting.

Melissa pulled me toward one of the bedrooms. "I was ... was thinking about what you said a couple weeks ago ... that Mason wasn't good in bed."

I slapped a hand over her mouth, trying to stop her from fucking yelling. If Mason found out ...

"Stop talking so damn loud."

Her lips moved against my palm, and I pulled it away so she could continue. She stopped by one of the last doors and clutched the handle. I stared at it, heart pounding against my chest. She had something planned, and I didn't know if I was going to like it.

"I thought I'd find you someone who could!"

She pushed the door open, and my jaw dropped to the fucking floor.

"Melissa, what the fuck?"

She was insane.

Victor sat on the bed, smoking a joint by himself, two unopened cans of beer sitting next to him. "About damn time you showed up," he said to Melissa. "Come here."

Melissa pushed me into the room and shut the door behind us. "Vicky ..." she said, plopping down next to him and drawing her fingers across his chest. "I want you to show Mia a good time."

A look of confusion crossed Victor's face, mirroring mine.

What the fuck is even happening? Why is she doing this?

Melissa kissed his neck and trailed her hands down his torso to the front of his pants. She gripped his bulge through them and looked at me. "Come here, Mia. It's okay."

"No," I said, backing away to the door. My heart was pounding in my chest, and my mind was all over the place. All I wanted to do was cry—hard. "I have Mason."

She hopped up from the bed, breasts bouncing in her tight white tank top, and pushed me toward the bed with him. "Mason doesn't do anything for you. Try it with Victor, please, for me?"

"He is your fucking boyfriend!" I said, turning around on my heel, angry as hell. "I'm not going to fuck him. What is wrong with you?"

She rolled her blue eyes and continued to push me until I stumbled back onto the bed. "Mia, it's fine. I don't mind. We have threesomes all the time."

Though they had *threesomes all the time*, Victor didn't make a move to touch me. Instead, he sat up on the bed, opened his beer, and chugged it, whispering something under his breath. It seemed like he didn't like this idea—or had known much about it —either.

"I don't want to have a threesome," I said, trying to get it through her head.

She smiled sweetly at me. "Well then, I'll leave you two alone." She hurried out the door and slammed it shut.

My eyes widened, and I shot up from the bed before Victor could try anything.

He held his hands up in defense. "I'm not going to do anything to you. I didn't even know she was going to bring you up." He puffed on his joint, then handed it to me. "You wanna hit?"

Tears welled up in my eyes, and I shook my head. I knew I shouldn't have come. I should've stayed at the hospital, should've gone out to eat or something—by myself. I shook my head at him and wanted to ask if he could take me to the hospital, but he continued to chug his beer.

I hurried back out through the door. "I have to go," I said, a tear falling down my cheek.

I grabbed my phone from my back pocket, then reached for my wallet to see if I had enough for a bus ride.

But my wallet was gone, my phone had five percent battery, my boyfriend was so drunk that he was almost passed out by the pool, and it was starting to drizzle outside.

Tears began streaming down my face, and I looked all over for my wallet, pushing people out of the way to check the floors, looking on all of the tables and counters for it, but I found nothing. Absolutely nothing.

Bad turned to worse, and I felt so goddamn alone. I didn't really have anyone. I didn't have someone who could take me home. I didn't have someone to talk to about this. I didn't even have a damn good boyfriend.

I stepped out the front door in the rain and let the tears fall. I was alone. Completely and utterly alone.

CHAPTER 22

MICHAEL

Julie stared at me from across the table, giving me those *fuck me* eyes that she had been giving me all night and a tense smile that had asked me a million times where I had been the last month. I hadn't wanted to come tonight, but she'd asked me out last minute, and I'd needed a damn drink.

Mia had been on my mind all last night and today. I could barely think straight at work. All I could hear was her voice uttering those words over and over and over. *"I just want sex,"* which to me sounded more like, "I just wanted to *use you* for sex."

Those words had haunted me for years. Linda had made sure to burn that thought in my memory for over a fucking decade. I had never been good enough for her, only when she got horny and didn't have anyone to hook up with on the side. Then she wanted *to use me* for sex.

I knew Mia had spoken out of anger and fear and stress, but … it still hurt.

I took another sip of my wine and sighed to myself.

The waiter came over with a wide smile on his face. "Have you decided on dessert?" he asked, placing two takeout boxes of our food on the table.

Before I could decline, Julie smiled widely at him. "Yes, please. Do you have a menu?"

The waiter handed her the dessert menu, and I pushed my hand into my pants pocket, grasping my phone, wishing that Mia would text me. I hadn't gone to see her today like I should have if I wanted her to know that I was serious about this.

Melissa had mentioned they were off to another party, so I'd decided to keep my distance. All I wanted was to help Mia. I couldn't stand watching her get used by Mason. I couldn't stand listening to her sound so desperate on the phone with her father. I couldn't stand how hurt I felt that she didn't want my help.

It was a pride thing. It was embarrassment. It was sorrow.

It fucking hurt.

I wanted to help her, but I couldn't help someone who didn't want help. Mia had to decide what she wanted for herself.

"So," Julie started, gaze lifting to mine from the menu, "what do you want?"

"Anything is fine," I said, trying hard not to seem too uninterested.

Julie was a nice girl; she just wasn't for me.

She twisted the menu in my direction and pushed it toward me. "They have chocolate cake and cinnamon apple pie, ice cre—"

"Chocolate cake," I said to the waitress quietly.

I couldn't get my thoughts to stop racing.

After the waitress handed each of us a piece and departed, Julie let out an exasperated sigh and seized my fingers on the table. "Stop tapping them." She tilted her head at me, eyes softening. "What happened? Why won't you tell me?"

I clenched my jaw and pulled my hand away from hers. *Don't flip out on her, Michael. She has done nothing wrong.* I balled my hand into a fist and pushed it under the table. "It's personal."

"So personal that you couldn't message me?"

My jaw twitched. What was I even doing here? I should have stayed home or gone to the hospital to try to clear things up with Mia. Not gone out on a fucking date with someone I didn't even want to be with from the start.

My phone buzzed in my pocket, and my heart lurched in my chest. I gripped it through my pants pocket, hand itching to answer it because I knew it was Mia. Nobody would call me this late, except her.

But I wouldn't interrupt dinner to check my phone. I ...

The phone continued and continued to buzz. I pulled it out of my pocket to see Mia's name flash on the screen. And before I could stop myself, I answered it and put it to my ear.

It was rude.

But it was Mia.

"Hello?"

"Michael," Mia said, followed by the sound of something pounding around her—rain. "I know that you probably hate me right now, but I don't have anyone else to call. I ... I ... Melissa and Mason are drunk, and she tried to force me to hook up with someone at the party, and I can't get back to the hospital, and I—" Her words came out so quickly that I could barely hear what she was saying.

"Mia, slow down. What's wrong?"

"Mia?" Julie seethed. She was giving me a look that I had only ever seen Melissa's mother give me before—pure wrath. "Who is Mia?"

I took a deep breath. "What's wrong?" I asked Mia again.

There was silence on the other end of the phone, and I could hear her choppy breaths. "Oh," she said quietly. "You're ... out on a date."

My heart ached when I heard the disappointment in her voice. "Tell me what's wrong, and I—"

"No," she said quickly. "No, it's okay. I don't want to bother you. I'll walk home."

"It's pouring outside," I said, glancing at the weather out the window.

"Have a nice date. Sorry for bothering you." And then the line went silent.

I gulped, trying to remember what party Melissa had said that she was going to tonight. Something had gone wrong, Melissa had fucked something up, and Mia had sounded so damn hurt.

I pulled out a few bills from my wallet and threw them on the table. I stood and grabbed my suit jacket. "I have to go," I said to Julie, stuffing my wallet back into my pocket.

Her big eyes widened at me. "Now? We're about to start dessert."

I glanced down at our table, the to-go boxes set to the side, the piece of cake she so desperately wanted to share in the middle, the glass of unfinished wine I knew she didn't really like but drank because I did. "Everything is paid for, Julie. Don't worry about it. It was great seeing you again."

Without even saying good-bye to her, I pushed through the door and ran out to my car through the rain. Maybe I was a fool. Maybe Mia really wanted me for sex and nothing more. But even then, I would still go pick her up because I didn't want her falling into a loveless relationship with someone, like I had. I wanted to see her happy. I wanted *her*.

CHAPTER 23

MIA

The rain beat down on my back, and I tried to shield my eyes from the harsh drops. One of those big green signs appeared in front of me, and I squinted up at it. *Mercy Hospital: 3 miles.* I curled my arms around my body, so I wouldn't heave back and forth.

What was wrong with me? Crying over Michael now because he had gone out on a date? I deserved all this damn pain. I had driven him away. I'd told him that there wasn't anything between us when I wanted there to be. He deserved to find a woman who wasn't as fucked up as I was, who didn't have so many problems that even she couldn't keep them straight.

Cars zoomed past me on the highway, their bright lights blinding me. One hit a pothole and sprayed me with all the water inside of it. I continued, not giving a single fuck anymore. All I wanted was to wash off in the hospital bathroom, change into a pair of fresh pajamas, and cry myself to sleep in the waiting room.

I walked for another fifteen minutes, which ended up being only a quarter mile, and thought about hitchhiking. It would surely be better than walking through this part of town this late at night.

A car pulled up to the side of the road, and I glanced back at it to see the shiny bright lights beaming at me. Someone got out, and I continued to hurry down the grass on the side of the busy freeway. Okay, maybe hitchhiking was a no-go. I didn't want to get into the car with a creepy, old—

"Mia?"

My heart dropped. I stopped dead in my tracks and turned around, seeing his figure in front of the headlights. Michael ... Michael was here. Michael was here for me.

"Mia, please, come home with me."

Though part of me wanted to protest and tell him to go back to his date, I ... I didn't have it in me to break him again. So, I walked toward him, wrapped my arms around his waist, and pulled him into a tight hug, burying my face into his chest.

"I'm sorry," I cried. "I'm sorry. I'm so sorry."

He wrapped his arms around me, brushing his fingers against my wet hair. "It's okay," he said softly.

But it wasn't okay, and I wasn't okay. Nothing about this was okay. He was my best friend's dad, showing me more affection and more love than my boyfriend did, more than my dad did, more than anyone—except Mom—did.

"Let me take you back to my place, Mia," he said. "You can stay with me tonight, and I'll bring you to see your mother tomorrow morning."

After swallowing all those emotions—hate, anger, sadness—that I had come to know so damn well, I nodded. "Okay." I walked to the passenger side and peered at the seat, not wanting to ruin his car with my wet clothes. "Do you want me to take off my wet—"

"Get in," he said.

I slid into the car and shut the door, listening to the rhythmic beat of the rain on the windshield. He started the car and veered back onto the road, merging onto the highway.

I stared down at my knees and frowned. "I'm sorry for ruining your date."

"You didn't ruin my date," he said. "I hadn't even wanted to go."

"Was it that girl you were at the bar with?" I asked before I could stop myself.

It didn't matter who the girl was. He didn't have to tell me if he didn't want to. I had hurt him.

His grip on the steering wheel tightened. "Don't do this, Mia," he said. "Don't try to make yourself hurt worse."

I stared at the windshield. "Okay, sorry."

And then I didn't say anything else for the rest of the car ride. I just enjoyed the silence because it was better than any music-blaring party I had ever attended.

When we reached his house, he led me to his bedroom, turned on the shower, and stripped off my clothes. "Get in."

I stepped into the shower, letting the water warm my bare and already-drenched skin. "The shower is big enough for two of us," I said, joking and trying to start a conversation again with him.

There was something about him tonight that seemed different from the usual talkative, friendly Michael. He had that strained look on his face like he had on Thursday right before he told me he wanted to give me money.

"Not now." He took a deep breath and walked out of the bathroom.

I listened to him fumbling around in his closet and closed my eyes. It felt like all I had been doing these past two weeks was cry, yet I felt like I needed to cry more. But I held it in and washed my hair with his shampoo and then my body with some soap.

About ten minutes later, Michael came back into the room

with some clothes and a fresh towel. He placed them on the sink counter and leaned against it, crossing his arms over his chest.

I stared at him, waiting for him to say something, but he didn't. Instead, he continued to stare at me with those intense gray eyes, and I continued to stand there, unsure about everything. After washing the soap off my body, I turned the water off and reached my hand out of the shower for the towel.

"What happened at the party?" he asked me.

I sucked in a deep breath, gazed at my feet, and wiggled my toes.

He grasped my chin and forced me to look up at him. "What happened?"

"I didn't even want to go," I whispered. My stomach tightened, and I didn't know if I should rat Melissa out to her own father or keep my friend's drama to myself. But after a few moments, I sighed. "Melissa ... made me feel uncomfortable."

He arched a brow. "What did she do?"

I tightened the towel around my torso. "She, um, asked me to sleep with her boyfriend."

Michael clenched his jaw even harder. He parted his lips, pressed them back together, and furrowed his brows, looking me up and down. "Did you?"

"No! I would never sleep with Victor. But she was so adamant, and ..." I shook my head. "I didn't have anyone who could take me back to the hospital, and I didn't know what to do. She had never acted like that before. I was ... scared." I shook my head yet again. "I'm sorry I just left her there."

A heap of guilt washed over me. God, I wasn't only a bad girlfriend to Mason and a bad *thing* to Michael, but I was also a bad friend to Melissa. I had left her at a party, drunk out of her fucking mind, with guys who wanted to fuck her senseless. I should've stayed and made sure she got home all right instead of running out like the loser I was.

Michael sighed deeply through his nose. "Melissa," he

muttered under his breath, rubbing the creases in his forehead with his index finger and thumb.

I wrapped the towel around myself, wiping the beads of water off my chest. "I should've stayed and made sure she was okay, not left."

What was wrong with me? I was a mess. I had family problems, boyfriend problems, friend problems, every freaking problem I could think of ... and I had no way of solving any of them. I continued to dig myself deeper and deeper into a hole.

"Victor texted me earlier. She's with him. Don't worry about her."

Someone knocked on the front door, and my stomach tightened. He had company this late at night? Maybe ... maybe I should leave and get out of his hair. He didn't need someone like me fucking up the rest of his life.

He handed me a spare change of clothes—his shirt and sweatpants—and excused himself. I finished drying myself off, stared at my puffy red eyes in the mirror, and got dressed. I parted my lips and thought about what I should do to excuse myself without being rude about it.

I'd already ruined one of his dates tonight.

After coming up with some lame excuses and deciding that they wouldn't cut it, I hung the towel on the hook and walked downstairs to find him. Ready to tell him that I was leaving, I parted my lips ... but then I stopped.

Michael stood at the bar with a box of pizza, a bottle of wine, and two wine glasses. He looked over at me, eyes drifting down my body and then back up it, and the smallest smile crawled onto his face. "You look good in my clothes, Mia."

"I, um ..." My cheeks flushed, and in that moment, I made the one decision that would change my life forever.

I wasn't going to leave. I wanted to stay with him—for more than the night. He had done so much for me that Mason wouldn't have ever done. He had stayed with me, even when I'd told him he didn't have to. He made a damn effort, and I had been nothing but a bitch to him.

I hopped down the last stair and smiled at him. "Thank you."

CHAPTER 24

MIA

After handing me a glass of wine, he brought the bottle and the pizza to the coffee table.

"Sit," he said.

I walked over to the couch and plopped down onto it.

He sat next to me and grabbed a slice. "We need to talk."

The words I had been dreading this entire night.

"About what?" I asked, trying not to burn my tongue on the cheese.

He raised a brow at me and cleared his throat. I expected him to say something along the lines of *You know exactly what we need to talk about*, but instead, he asked, "Are you okay?"

I raised my brows at him, surprised at the question, and stuffed the slice in my mouth, not caring how hot it was. I took some time to chew and to calm myself down. "I'm fine. Tonight was just—"

"I'm not talking about tonight." He paused for a moment. "I

never asked you if you were okay. I doubt anyone did after what happened to your mother."

My gaze fell to the wine glass, and I picked it up. Thinking about the whole situation made me feel like becoming a damn drunk because I felt so helpless. I drew my finger across the rim. "It's happened before," I said. "I dealt with it then, and I'll deal with it now."

"How?"

"Why do you have so many damn questions?"

"Because ..." He paused for a moment and stared at me with the most confident expression I had ever seen. "I care about you." He didn't stumble on his words. He didn't act like he didn't give a single fuck. He said the words and meant them, and I could feel it.

The air sat, thick with tension, and I stared back at him, not knowing how *I* felt about hearing him say it. Something about it felt so freeing, like I didn't have to do anything alone, like he would always be there for me ...

"How are you going to deal with it?" he asked again, placing his glass of wine on the coffee table and turning in my direction.

I took a deep breath and glanced down at my thighs. I was going to have to continue using Mason for money, so I could survive. It was the only way. I didn't want to be a damn charity case to anyone else. So, I shrugged my shoulders. "I can't do anything now. When she gets out of intensive care and can leave the hospital ..." My voice got quiet, and I gulped. *Where will she go?*

I had researched some places when I had time, but they were way too expensive.

"When she gets out, I'm going to get an apartment and take care of her."

Mason wouldn't want that trouble all the time. He didn't have the patience, and I didn't trust anyone else.

"What about your studies? Your job?"

I shrugged again. "I don't know. I'll have to take time off."

He sighed deeply through his nose. "When she gets out of the hospital ... I know this place about an hour north of the city. My father stays there. The nurses take good care of the patients."

"What's the name?" I asked.

"St. Barbars."

"That's way out of my price range." Hell, everything was. "I can't afford that."

"I can," he said, staring me straight in the eye. I parted my lips, about to refuse any type of monetary help from him, when he shook his head. "Don't start. I would've done this years ago, if you had told me then. It's not because I'm trying to win you over, and I'm not going to make you pay me back or even feel like you have to."

"But—"

"I didn't bring this up to argue about it. It isn't a question that I need your answer to." He looked me dead in the eyes. "I'm going to help you whether you accept my money or not."

I was going to open my mouth again to say something, but then I pressed my lips back together. It hurt me so damn much to not say anything. It hurt me to be silent about this because I didn't want his money. But that look in his eyes told me that he wasn't going to give up. He would continue to push and push until I caved.

And by that time ... I'd be drowning in debt from hospital bills.

"Promise me two things," I said, grabbing his hands. "Don't treat me any differently than you have been. I don't want to be a charity case. I just want to be ... be with you like this. And ... don't do anything finances-wise with my mom behind my back."

He smiled. "I would never treat you differently, Mia."

My heart felt warm and fuzzy, and I smiled. It felt so weird to have someone show me that they cared and actually meant it. I'd never thought it'd happen—ever—in this lifetime. I sank into the couch next to him and stared at the TV show he'd turned on while I had been getting ready. But instead of watching it, I grinned to myself. As weird and messed up as this whole situation was ... I was falling for my best friend's dad.

We must've sat there for hours, and I found myself curled up into him, his arm around me, my head resting on his shoulder, his scent drifting through my nose. It was the most peace I'd had in ... probably ever.

Mason and I never did this. Maybe we had when we first started dating, but even then, he always tried to get into my pants mid-movie.

My eyes closed. This was what I wanted. This was what I'd dreamed of for so damn long. Being happy with someone, even when the world was dragging me down. Feeling free. Loving —*loving?* My heart skipped a beat, and I gulped.

Did ... did I just think loving?

I sat back up, the word replaying through my mind. I glanced over at Michael, who looked down at me, his hand drifting from my shoulder to my knee.

"This is how it could be every night with me," Michael said, resting his hand on my thigh and squeezing.

Something about the way he touched me so tenderly made me feel *things*.

Tingles ran up and down my legs, and my heart beat a bit faster. I parted my lips and took a deep breath, trying to erase the thought of loving him. It made my stomach tighten because it was a damn scary word that both Dad and Mason used on me to get me to break for them.

"I'm not like Mason or your father," he said, fingers gently rubbing against my inner thigh. "I'm not going to hurt you. I'm not going to leave when it gets hard. I'm not going to flirt with other women or ignore you when you need me."

God, I wanted this more than anything. He was so damn sincere, so damn caring. I knew I wouldn't find someone like him ever, ever again. But even if I dumped Mason, I didn't know if this would work.

"Michael, we can't. What would we say to Melissa? She'd ... she'd hate me for being with her dad. I know that she wouldn't talk to me ever again as soon as she found out."

Michael clenched his jaw. "So, what do you suggest we do? Sneak around together late at night, hoping we don't get caught by someone else?"

I placed my hands against his chest, curling my fingers into it. "I don't know." I really didn't.

We were stuck because this was so much more than physical now. I ... I had feelings for him. And I knew that he had feelings for me.

A look of hurt crossed his face, but then it was replaced with anger. "Do you really only want me for sex?" he asked, gray eyes so icy that I had to take a sharp breath.

I knew that he knew that wasn't all I wanted. I wouldn't have called him earlier tonight, and I wouldn't have stayed for this long at his house; I would've gotten up and left.

"No," I said quietly, looking down at my lap. I couldn't even believe I had said that to him yesterday. It was so wrong of me to even put the words out there. I ... I didn't think it would hurt him. But at that time, I hadn't been thinking about anyone hurting, except myself.

"Look at me when you talk, Mia," he said, his voice stern.

I glanced up at him. "No, I don't want you for only sex."

The pure intensity of his eyes was enough to make me want to look back down. I could feel him about to say something ... say something that I wished he wouldn't.

"Prove it to me."

"How do you want me to prove it to you? What do you want me to do?"

He paused for a long moment, then handed me my phone that I had put on the coffee table. "Break up with Mason."

CHAPTER 25

MIA

I stared between him and the phone, nerves zipping through me. *Break up with Mason?* If I broke up with Mason and if I trusted Michael with my entire life ... things could go very, very wrong. I didn't want to be with Mason at all, but he was safe. He'd been helping me for years, and I knew he'd continue.

Being with Michael, hiding our relationship from Melissa ... that was sticky and more than risky. What if Melissa found out and drove us apart? Michael would choose her over me any day of the fucking week. She was his daughter.

He growled lowly under his breath. "Maybe sex *is* all you want."

"No, Michael," I breathed out. "It's not all I want ..."

He moved his fingers up the inside of my thigh, higher and higher and higher.

"But ..."

He brushed two fingers against the front of my pants, moving them gently. "But?"

I took a shaky breath, knowing exactly what he was doing.

"But you just want this ..."

He grabbed my ankles, pulled me fully onto the couch, and spread my legs. Then, he pulled down the pants I wore, lay between my legs, and rested my thighs on his shoulders. I stared down at him, my breath catching in the back of my throat. He spread my folds and pressed his tongue against my clit, drawing it in small circles.

I clenched, the force building inside me. God, this was damn good ... but I wanted more of him. I really did. He stared up at me with icy-gray eyes.

"Close your eyes," he said. "Think about the last time Mason made you feel this good."

My eyes fluttered closed. I didn't picture Mason, instead thinking about being with Michael every night. He had promised me once before that he'd take care of me, that he'd be there for me no matter what, and he had proven to me that he wouldn't give up on me. I arched my back, slipped my hand into his hair, and moved my hips back and forth against him.

His breath heated my folds, and his tongue hit my clit in just the right spot. I curled my toes, my legs starting to tremble. He set his lips harder against my clit, ravenously eating my pussy, and pushed a finger inside of me. I moaned at the sudden tension, my pussy immediately wrapping around his finger like it was the biggest thing that had ever been inside of me.

"More," I moaned.

He pushed another finger inside of me, pumping them in and out quickly. I threw my head back, my breasts bouncing in his shirt each time he moved his fingers inside of me. I let out another moan, and he continued to eat my pussy until I was close to coming.

My legs were trembling, my heart pounding in my chest. As I

was about to come, he'd slow down, mix up his pace, pull his fingers out of me, make me desperate. When I whined, desperate for more, he'd start back up, tugging on my nipple, breathing on my wetness, sucking my clit between his lips. And then he'd stop, refusing to let me come.

"More, Michael …" I stared down into his eyes and furrowed my brows, a surge of pleasure rushing through me. "Please, give me more."

He kissed up my folds to my hips, letting his lips linger on my skin before crawling closer to me and grinding his bulge against my aching pussy. He set his lips against my jaw, sucking harshly on the skin. "Is this why you called me to come pick you up tonight?"

He ground himself into me, and I reached between us, unable to stop myself, and thrust my hand into his suit pants to grab his cock. I stroked it and pressed the head against my entrance. Though it was through his pants, my body ached for him to push it inside of me.

"Harder," I begged.

He pushed against me, and heat gathered in my pussy.

God, I needed him inside of me. So. Damn. Bad.

"Please, give it to me."

He wrapped his hand around the front of my throat, pulled my upper body off the couch, and pushed down his pants. Then, he shoved himself into me without warning. His dick slid into me with ease. My eyes widened as I adjusted to his size, and I moaned out loud. He pulled me toward him with each thrust, my breasts against his bare chest. He tugged on my nipple—hard—through my shirt.

"Oh my God," I said under my breath, eyes rolling back. The pressure was driving me higher than it ever had before.

The angry, dark Michael had finally come out to play.

"Harder, Michael. Give it to me harder."

He pulled out of me, and I whimpered, my whole body

needing him more than I'd needed anything ever. Before I could react, he turned me onto my stomach and plunged himself back into me from behind. My fingers curled into the couch cushions. He grabbed a fistful of my hair in one hand and slapped my phone down on the couch next to me.

"If this is all you want, call your boyfriend and tell him to pick you up after I finish fucking you senseless ..." he said into my ear, his voice tense. "Or tell him that you're done with him."

My heart raced in my chest, and my cheeks flushed. He didn't give me another choice. Mason or him. My boyfriend or my best friend's dad.

He pumped into me, and I closed my eyes.

"No," I said through gritted teeth, trying to hold back my orgasm. It was selfish and—

Almost as if it were fate, Mason's name flashed on the screen. Before I could end the call, Michael tapped on it to answer it, and I held a hand to my mouth to muffle my moans.

Why was he calling me now?

Michael slipped an arm around my waist and rubbed my pussy with his fingers. I took a shaky breath, trying to calm myself.

"Babe?" Mason asked.

I could hear my damn heart pounding in my ears.

"Babe, where'd you go?"

"Didn't even notice you were gone for hours," Michael growled into my ear.

My pussy tightened on him, and he played with it, driving me closer and closer to the edge. The tension rose in my core, and I squeezed my eyes closed.

Calm down, Mia. Calm down.

"Go ahead, Mia ..." Michael taunted. "Tell him to pick you up. Tell him why you're here with me."

My mind buzzed with so many thoughts. He tightened his grip in my hair and pumped into me.

"Mia?" Mason asked, voice filled with *worry*. "What the hell was that?"

Michael rubbed my pussy faster.

"Mason ..." I breathed.

If Michael didn't stop ... I was going to ...

"Mason, I—"

Michael slapped my clit, and I screamed out, coming all over his cock. My whole body was trembling, my eyes rolling back into my head, my pussy lips pulsing over and over on him.

"Are you touching yourself?" Mason asked.

"She's getting fucked, you fucking idiot," Michael said over my shoulder. "This is how she sounds when she's coming."

The tension built inside me even more, and he slapped my clit over and over and over, sending me higher yet again.

"In case you wanted to know."

Mason started yelling over the phone, threatening Michael that he would have his ass. But I sank into the couch and let Michael continue to fuck me senseless, like he'd promised.

"Mason," I breathed out. "Mason, we're over."

CHAPTER 26

MICHAEL

"Mason," she said, her voice raspy. Though I had known she wanted to keep us a secret and I'd ruined that for her, I didn't know what I was expecting her to say to him, but it wasn't ... "Mason, we're over."

I thought my heart had stopped for a moment. I stilled inside of her and felt her clench on my cock, whimpering under me. Mason's voice rang through the phone; he was screaming at her and calling her every name in the book, asking who she was with and how she could just drop him after everything he had done for her.

My lips brushed against the back of her neck, and I realized that *I* was in the wrong. I had forced her to make a decision she hadn't wanted to make, and she'd had to break up with him. She shut off the phone and tossed it away from the couch.

"Don't stop," she breathed, her voice quiet. "Please, don't stop."

I pulled myself out of her, turned her around, and pushed some hair out of her face. I couldn't believe that she had actually done it—that I had made her do it—and I didn't know how exactly I felt about it. Was it wrong? It didn't feel wrong.

"Michael," she whispered.

I took a steady breath through my nose and pressed my lips to hers, driving myself back into her. She wrapped around me, like she wanted me more than anything.

"Say my name again, Mia," I mumbled against her lips.

She dug her fingers into my chest, and I inhaled her sweet scent.

"Michael." Her voice was gentle, and I pressed my lips harder to hers, thrusting in and out of her faster. All she had to say was my name to drive me wild and over the edge.

I had never had a woman choose me—*really* choose me—like that.

It felt good and freeing, and I hoped to God that Mia felt the same way about me as I did about her because this feeling wasn't going away anytime soon. I didn't care about Melissa knowing. All I wanted was to make Mia happy. She deserved it even though she didn't think so. She was one of the sweetest, most caring, selfless people I knew.

Unlike my ex-wife, unlike Julie. Mia was different.

Her fingers curled into my hair, and she tugged on it. Her hips moved with mine, her hands holding me close to her. I trailed my fingers up her side and wrapped my hand around the back of her neck to draw her even closer because I couldn't keep myself away.

Faster, I pumped into her, feeling her grip down around me and tense in my embrace. She cried out against my lips, and a tear fell down her cheek. So many emotions were spilling out of her, and I slowed down.

"No," she said. "Please, don't stop again."

So, I hesitantly continued until I was about to explode. I wiped a stray tear from Mia's cheek with my thumb and was about to pull out of her to come on her stomach when she wrapped her legs around my waist and pulled me down to her.

"Come inside of me," she said.

I groaned in her ear and rested my forehead against hers, coming inside of her. She lightly moved her fingers over my jaw and gave me a sad smile. I took a deep breath, pulled her against my chest, and rolled us over until she was lying on me.

She stared down at me through huge brown eyes with tears streaming down her face, and I pushed each one away. I didn't know how to feel. Part of me wanted to feel so damn good about breaking her and Mason up, but the other half of me was devastated that I had stooped so low to get Mia to make a difficult decision for herself. I had been the cause of these tears. I'd made her vulnerable.

"Michael," she said. She grabbed my hand and placed it firmly on her chest, right above her heart, her fingers intertwined with mine. "I am so scared." Her voice wasn't more than a whisper. "What if he tries to do something to Mom? What if …" I could hear the questions coming right off her lips before she even said it. "What if something happens between us"—more tears—"and I end up on the streets?"

Her chest was rising and falling so harshly that I pulled her to me and refused to let her sit back up.

"Calm down, Mia," I said into her ear. "Nothing will happen between us."

"But-but what if … what if it does?" Her cries turned into hiccups. "You don't know what will happen, and I don't want to end up homeless with Mom. I won't be able to support her. I can't afford all these bills. I don't have anyone to help me."

"Mia, I promise you that I won't let that happen," I said.

Even if whatever we had ended between us and if Mia wanted nothing to do with me, I would never let her live alone on the streets. It wasn't the type of person I had been for the last thirty-eight years. I'd be damned if I started to act like that now.

I could still feel the tension in her entire body, unsure if I was telling the truth, scared that I would leave her, terrified that I'd be another one of the men who treated her like garbage.

I pushed some hair out of her face and smiled up at her. "You have to promise me something too."

She paused for a moment. "What?" she asked quietly.

The words almost didn't come out. As much as I wanted to keep Mia forever, I didn't want her to ever feel the way Mason had made her feel. I wanted her to be happy wherever she was or whoever she ended up with.

I sucked in a deep breath and parted my lips. "If you ever feel like you don't want to be with me, please don't lead me on. I know you had reasons to lead Mason on—not that he really respected you anyway—but if you don't want me anymore, just tell me." I could feel the heat crawling up my neck, and all those bad memories with Melissa's mother ran through my mind.

Being broken up with was tough, even when you didn't love the person anymore. But … being lied to about how someone truly felt … thinking that you were the world to someone, only to find out that they hadn't felt like that about you for so long … that hurt so much more. And I didn't want it to happen again. I couldn't let it happen again.

"I will help you as much as you need even if you want to end it with me. Just don't lead me on."

Her hesitant eyes softened, and she curled her fingers into my chest, nodding her head. "Okay," she whispered, bottom lip quivering. "I promise not to lead you on." A strand of brown hair fell into her face. "I promise to give you my all, and … I promise to trust you."

CHAPTER 27

MIA

The next morning, I woke up in Michael's bed with his arms wrapped around me, his nose in my hair, and his husky voice in my ear.

"Morning," he mumbled, pulling me closer.

I took a deep breath, opened my eyes to stare at the cracked window, and smiled.

After our conversation last night and after crying my eyes out some more, I finally felt good about us. It was so difficult to trust him after what Dad had done to Mom and me and after what Mason—I was almost sure of—had done to me too. But Michael had proven to me time and time again that he wasn't like Dad or Mason. He actually cared about me. And it was refreshing to wake up to someone who didn't smell like another girl's perfume.

"I need to go see Mom today," I said.

He kissed below my ear. "Let me take you out to breakfast first."

I rolled over to face him and smiled, watching his tired eyes open. "How about we get breakfast on the way?" I asked, pushing a strand of his hair off his forehead.

I didn't want to waste much time anywhere else. This was the longest time I had spent away from Mom since she had gone back into the hospital, and I didn't like the thought of Mason getting there to tell her what I had done before I did.

Something in the pit of my stomach told me that Mason was about to freak out—more than he already had. Maybe it was that he'd left text message after text message on my phone last night, calling me a slut and whore and saying that I would never find someone else like him. Maybe it was that deep down, I knew he was a terrible guy. He always had been, and he always would be.

And besides, I didn't want anyone finding out about Michael and me yet. All that had to happen was for one frat guy or sorority girl to see me out with Michael, and Melissa would find out. This city was big, but everyone seemed to know someone here.

His fingers curled into my hips, and I felt so warm. "One day, Mia."

"One day." I held out my pinkie, and he wrapped his around it and chuckled. "I promise."

After I dressed in some clothes that I'd left in Melissa's bedroom for sleepovers when we were in high school, I hurried to the car, where Michael was waiting for me. I stared down at my phone during the whole ride, my stomach tightening in knots, and sipped on my coffee. To my surprise, Mason hadn't texted me this morning, and I didn't know if that was a good thing or a bad thing.

When we drove into the hospital parking lot, my stomach dropped. Mason's car was parked in one of the spaces. Michael parked right goddamn next to him, and I tried to shrink down in my seat, so if Mason was still in his car, he wouldn't see me.

"Relax, Mia," Michael said. "He's not there."

I placed a hand on his shoulder and sipped my coffee. "Let me go in first. Come in five minutes after me or something. If we go in together, he'll be suspicious," I said.

Michael looked at me, giving me that *let him be suspicious* look. But I shook my head.

"If he finds out, he'll tell Melissa, and I want to tell her myself." Though ... I didn't know how the fuck I was going to do that or *if* it would happen anytime soon.

Michael tensed for a moment, his jaw twitching, but then he sighed. "Fine. I'll wait."

I took a deep breath, readying myself to face the devil himself, and walked into the hospital. I didn't know what I was going to say or do when I saw him, but I knew that he was about to start a fight with me.

After stepping onto the elevator, I squeezed my eyes closed and tried to steady my breathing. It was hot in here, and my breaths were coming out in short little gasps. The doors opened, and I immediately locked eyes with him.

Sitting in the waiting room with Melissa and Serena, he clenched his jaw and stood up. His eyes looked like pure fire, blazing and trying to burn me. He snatched my upper arm roughly in his hand and pulled me into the hallway.

"What the fuck?" he growled, nostrils flaring, eyes hard. "Who the fuck were you with last night?"

I pressed my lips together. "Nobody that you need to worry about," I said more confidently than I'd thought I would. But I was getting damn tired of Mason treating me this way. "We're over."

"We're not fucking over, Mia." He tightened his grip around my arm until it started to tingle. "Who the fuck was it? I'm going to kill the bastard with my own two hands," he growled, not even giving me time to utter a comeback. "You know, I didn't know you were such a whore, sleeping with another man while you were with me. Taking *my* money for your mother. Using me to get what you wanted."

I gulped and attempted not to think of Dad saying all these things to Mom while I watched helplessly when I was a child. *Mason isn't good for me. He really isn't good for me.* I had to make sure I repeated that over and over and over, so I didn't become like Mom.

"I'm not a whore," I said.

He chuckled menacingly. "Yes, you are. You fucked me for the past five years for money."

"I never asked you to spend money on me. You offered to help my mom."

"Because I fucking loved you ..." He shook his head, as if he did nothing wrong. "And you had to go cheat on me with someone else. You're a gold-digging whore, Mia. Nothing more. No other guy would ever put up with all of your shit."

I bit my tongue and held back my angry tears.

"I am the only one who could put up with all of your nagging and all of your crying and bitching. All of these damn bills you have." He shook his head again, glaring down at me and trying to turn this back on me.

And if I hadn't known any better, then I would've let him. But ... I now knew how I wanted to be treated, and it wasn't like this. It was how Michael treated me—with respect.

I ripped my arm away from him and narrowed my eyes. "Well, maybe if you'd paid attention to me and shown me some respect instead of flirting with a bunch of other girls, things would've been different."

"Maybe if you didn't fake it in bed, I wouldn't have to flirt with other women to get off."

I stepped closer to him, my jaw tightened so it wouldn't twitch in pure rage. "If you could actually get me to come, I wouldn't have to fake it!" I shouted at him.

Everyone in the entire hallway froze and looked over at us, but I didn't care. I was angry and sad and so fucking stressed out. And this man was driving me insane. I didn't want to deal with this right now. Hell, I didn't want to deal with his stupid, sorry ass at all.

Mason grabbed my arm again, fingers digging harshly into it. "Your mother won't have a place to stay when she gets out of the hospital. You'll be living on the streets without fucking food or a place to clean yourself. A dirty fucking whore. You know, I was actually thinking about giving you a second chance, Mia. I don't want to see your mother with no place to live ... but you won't stop being a bitch, and I don't need that in my life."

I raised my brows at him and stepped back. "Well then, leave. I'm not stopping you."

He slammed his fist right into the wall beside my head, turned on his heel, and stormed toward the elevator. "Have fun being a homeless fucking bitch," he said and walked right into the elevator.

CHAPTER 28

MIA

As soon as the elevator doors closed, I slumped my shoulders forward and felt so relaxed. It felt like the world had been lifted off my shoulders, and I could finally breathe again. It wasn't really how I'd wanted that argument to go—because I knew he'd try to break me—but it was better than getting back together with him.

I walked into the waiting room, knowing that Melissa and Serena had heard every word of our conversation. Hell, the whole hospital probably had. I hoped Mom's door was closed and that she hadn't heard a word of it because that would hurt so much more than anything Mason could say to me.

"Are you okay?" Serena asked.

I slumped down in a chair next to her and rested my head on her shoulder. I didn't have any more tears for that man, and I was glad.

Serena skimmed her fingers against my forearm. "He wasn't good for you anyway."

"Yeah," Melissa said, trying to lighten the mood. "Tell us about this man you went home with last night."

I hoped that Michael didn't walk in anytime soon because … I didn't know how I'd get any words out with him smirking at me from across the room. All I would think about was last night and the way he'd touched me so savagely as I talked to Mason.

"Um …" I said, rubbing my palms on my jeans. "I don't even remember his name."

Melissa rolled her eyes. "Ugh, don't give us that. He had to be damn good if he got you to break up with Mason. So, who was he?" she asked. Then, her lips curled into a smile. "Was it Victor?! Maybe another guy?"

Serena furrowed her brows. "Why would she fuck your boyfriend?"

I rolled my eyes and gave Serena my best *you will never believe what happened at the party* look.

But Melissa clapped her hands together, completely ignoring it. "I knew he'd be good for you."

"It wasn't Victor," I said.

Melissa rolled her blue eyes and made a face. "Then, who was it?" She turned to Serena and narrowed her eyes. "Do you know? You're awfully quiet."

Serena shook her head. "No."

Melissa looked at her phone flashing with text messages from Victor and rolled her eyes, yawning. "Victor wants me to come over." She walked to the elevator and waved at me from inside it. "Try to get it out of her, Serena," she said, winking at me.

And when the elevator doors closed, I blew out a deep breath through my nose. God, this was going to be so much harder than I'd thought it would be.

How did I even bring it up in conversation? Did I come out with it and say, *Oh, hey, Melissa, I'm doing your dad?*

"So," I said, "how is your boyfriend's sister's baby? Boy or girl?"

Serena slapped me on the arm. "First, she had a girl named Anna. And second, come on! Spill the damn tea! I've been in joy since I heard you broke up with Mason! What happened with *Michael?*"

I looked around the room to make sure there were no prying ears and said, "Lower your voice. I don't want anyone finding out yet."

And then I dived into everything that had happened within the past twenty-four hours—from when she'd left me at the party to Melissa trying to get me to hook up with Victor to Michael answering my phone call with Mason.

When I finished, she stared at me with wide eyes and her mouth opened. "Oh my God." She fanned herself and burst out laughing. "Oh my God! Mia! You got yourself a real man!" She jumped out of her seat and started pacing the waiting room with a huge grin on her face. "I don't even have damn words for it. You are living an actual fantasy!"

I raised my brows and glanced down the hall in the direction of Mom's room. "I don't know about that."

Serena sat back down next to me and grabbed my hands. "You know what I mean. Our best friend's dad ... you're, like, dating him now?"

Dating? I didn't know what we were exactly. "I guess you could say that."

Suddenly, the excited expression dropped from her face. "How are you going to tell Melissa? I don't know how she's going to take it, knowing that her best friend and her dad are getting it on in every corner of his house."

I sank down in my seat and groaned. "I don't know how to tell her. Do you think she's going to be angry with me?" I asked.

"To be honest, I would be angry if it were my dad. But ... Melissa has been in a better mood than usual lately. If you tell her soon, maybe she won't be as mad?" Serena shrugged her shoulders. "I don't know. That's a difficult decision."

Well, I had known it would be, but hearing it from Serena made it seem a hundred times worse than it was. "I … if she decides to end our friendship after all these years, will you stay by my side?" I asked. It felt weird, asking Serena, but … I didn't want to be alone in this. I needed someone to talk to now that Mason was out of the picture.

Serena rolled her eyes. "Oh, don't even ask me that! You know I will." She paused. "But … there's something I have to tell you." Her smile turned into a frown. "I don't want to stress you out even more, but …"

My heart dropped, as I thought about what she could say that would hurt me. It seemed this past month had already been absolute hell. I didn't know if I could take more.

"Mason is telling everyone that you're a whore," she said. "Everyone at the frat last night knows that you were being fucked by someone when you broke up with him." She wrapped her arms around me and brought me into a hug. "And you know that everyone is going to believe him."

While part of me hurt, I was starting not to give a single fuck about him anymore. I didn't care what a bunch of no-good, sleazy frat boys thought of me. They were immature assholes who cheated on their girlfriends all the damn time. I didn't need the extra drama in my life right now or at all.

Serena's gaze shifted from me to the elevator doors when they opened. She pulled away, and Michael walked out, one hand stuffed into his pocket, the other holding his coffee. He had a smug smirk on his face, and I wondered what had taken him so damn long to come up here. Maybe he had been talking to Melissa after I ratted on her last night … or maybe he had been talking to Mason.

Serena bumped her shoulder into mine and winked, walking toward the elevator to leave. "Have fun with Daddy Bryne."

CHAPTER 29

MIA

I stared down at my phone to read another text message from Mason, calling me a slut, and sighed. It had been only four days since I had broken up with him, but it felt like a damn lifetime. He hadn't left me alone like I'd thought he would, and he hadn't told me when I could come get my stuff.

But I knew one thing: I wasn't about to go back to his place alone. I didn't trust him.

The elevator doors opened, and I glanced up to see a smiling Michael walk through them with a brown paper bag that smelled like Italian grinders. He placed it down in front of me and went in for a kiss, but I moved my head away before he could.

"Not here," I said, glancing down the hallway to make sure nobody had seen us and unwrapping my grinder to eat it.

I watched him frown and felt bad about it, but he didn't complain. Instead, he sat down next to me and pulled out our dinner.

"I'm taking you out on a real date soon," he said to me.

I raised a brow at him. "I don't remember agreeing to that."

"You didn't." He smiled at me, his gray eyes lighting up with excitement.

My heart warmed, and I playfully rolled my eyes. "Only if Mom's surgery goes well."

"She's having surgery?"

"Scheduled for the day after tomorrow." I paused for a long moment and peered back down the hallway toward her room.

Since we had officially become a *thing*, I hadn't asked Michael to actually come into the room to see Mom with me. I didn't want her to think that something was up with us because it'd make her worry more. But I wanted her to get more comfortable with him around.

"Do you want to see her?" I asked him.

"Of course," he said.

I stuffed our half-eaten sandwiches back into the bag and nodded toward her room. My fingers brushed against his as we walked, tingles shooting up my arm. When Mom saw us through her window, she smiled and waved at us to come into the room.

Michael opened the door for me, and I inched my way inside, glad *I* wasn't hooked up to a monitor because my heart rate was through the damn roof. Michael followed me in, his hand on my back.

And Mom saw. She definitely saw.

"Michael, how are you?" she asked, smiling weakly.

Michael glanced at me, then back at her. "Doing good. What about yourself? Mia says that you'll be having surgery soon."

Mom waved at him. "Oh, it's nothing."

I walked over to her and sat at the end of her bed. "Mom, it's not nothing," I said.

Michael pulled a chair closer to her bed and sat down in it, his knee grazing against mine. I tensed for a moment, and then I looked back at Mom and relaxed.

"You're having brain surgery."

"I've had it before."

I shook my head. "So?"

"She's being optimistic, Mia." Michael squeezed my knee lightly, letting his hand linger.

Mom eyed us, then stared politely at Michael. "Michael, can I speak with my daughter alone for a moment?" Mom asked.

My heart raced.

Michael nodded and walked out of the room, sitting on one of the benches right outside.

Mom turned to me. "All right, spill. What's wrong?"

"Nothing's wrong, Mom."

"Don't lie to me, Mia."

I squeezed her hand, my heart hurting. It didn't feel good to lie, but I didn't want to tell Mom yet. She didn't need to stress over me and an older man, thinking she had to fret about me or ask me questions all the time if I was okay.

But then she asked, "What's going on with you and Mr. Bryne?"

She knew. She already knew.

"I, um …" I gulped and scooted closer to her. "We're together," I whispered. "And … I know it sounds bad. I know he's older than I am. But … but I think I love him."

Her eyes widened. "I knew there was something going on between you and him, but love?"

"I'm sorry," I said. "I haven't told him yet. I don't know how. I'm scared, and I don't want to be hurt again, but … he's so caring and sweet and loving. He's spent every night at the hospital with me while Mason barely could show up for five minutes."

Mom swept her thumb across my cheek. "Don't cry, sweetheart. Come here." She pulled me down in the bed with her and stroked my hair. "Mr. Bryne is a good man. I can tell, even from all the way in here, that he cares for you a lot."

I pressed my ear to her chest and listened to the steady rhythm of her heartbeat. "You're not mad?"

She laughed, her silky-smooth voice fluttering through my ears. "Of course not. I've been trying to keep up a good relationship with Mason because I know what he does for you and for us, but I've been hoping you'd break up with him. Saturday morning, he looked like he was going to kill someone. And from that one moment, I could tell that he wasn't the best guy for you since I came here. Did he ever care for you?"

My lips quivered, and I held her tighter, trying not to cry more because I felt like such a crybaby lately. But life was so fucking hard sometimes that I couldn't help it.

"No," I whispered. "He didn't."

"Why'd you stay with him?" she asked.

And those five little words broke my heart even more. If I told Mom, she'd be disappointed that I'd sacrificed my happiness for hers. She'd feel worse than she did now, and I didn't want that to happen, so I shrugged my shoulders and said, "I thought I loved him."

We stayed quiet for a few moments, and a tear fell down her cheek. "I know the feeling..." she said. "Your father made me feel so good when we started dating, but I didn't see that he was manipulative and abusive. I'm sorry for keeping you in that environment for so long." Her heart rate monitor sped up, and she sniffled.

She pulled away and furrowed her brows at me. "I know I shouldn't pry, but I have to ask ... Mr. Bryne didn't coerce you into anything you didn't want to do, did he?"

I smiled up at her and shook my head. "No," I said. "He didn't."

She lifted her gaze to the empty window. "Good. Now, why don't you go spend the night with him? I'll be having surgery in a couple days, and I would like to know that you haven't been up for the past forty-eight hours, agonizing about me."

"But—"

She lightly pushed me off the bed. "Go, Mia." She smiled. "I love you."

CHAPTER 30

MIA

"So, your mother?" Michael asked on our way back to his house.

The moon was glowing brightly up above, and I watched it as we drove down the desolate streets.

"Does she know?"

I took a deep breath through my nose and nodded. "Yes, and so does Serena."

He paused and stopped at a stoplight, glancing over at me. "I'm sorry. I shouldn't have made it obvious."

I grasped his face in my hands and pressed my lips to his. "It's okay. I don't mind them knowing."

I pulled away and tried to calm the butterflies in my stomach. Part of me wanted to just say those three little words to him right then and there, but I stopped myself. What if he didn't feel the same way yet? What if it was too soon?

"It's Melissa that I'm worried about," I said instead of confessing the feelings I had for him.

We sat in silence for the rest of the drive. I bounced my knees up and down, thinking about when it would be a good time to say it. I didn't have the slightest clue about how I should act in a normal relationship.

Michael pulled into his driveway, bright, blinding headlights lighting up the dark. And my stomach dropped almost immediately. Parked right in her usual spot was Melissa's car.

"I thought you said Melissa wasn't going to be here?" I whispered to him, my heart pounding against my chest.

Michael parked his car next to hers, cut the lights, and arched a brow. From the lights in the backyard, I could tell that Melissa was out in the back, probably in the pool with Victor.

"She didn't tell me she would be."

"We should leave," I said.

What would happen if she found me with her father? I didn't have an excuse for being here. I could probably think of something, but not anything believable.

Michael stared at me from the driver's seat and leaned closer. "Oh, come on, Mia. It's not like we haven't snuck around before." He slipped his hand between my legs and massaged my clit through my shorts.

And if I said it didn't turn me on, I'd be lying.

He moved closer until his lips were next to my ear, and then he slipped his fingers into my shorts, rubbing my pussy. "I know it excites you, Mia."

"It doesn't," I said.

He chuckled so menacingly in my ear. "Take off your shirt."

"Michael, no—"

"Take it off now, Mia," he said.

I gulped and took off my shirt, sitting in the passenger seat with just my lacy black bra on, the moonlight glistening against my breasts.

He took my shirt from me and hooked his finger around the bra strap. "This too."

"No, Melissa will see us."

"Melissa is in the pool," he said. "She won't see you."

"Are you being serious?" I asked in disbelief, the warmth pooling between my legs.

"My house, Mia. I make the rules."

I grumbled to myself, yet I did what I had been told because, well, I was too horny to throw a fit. I unclipped my bra, letting my breasts fall out of it, and handed it to him.

"Do you want me to take my shorts off too?" I asked sarcastically.

"I wasn't going to make you, but since you offered."

He held out his hand and waited for me to remove my jean shorts. I tried not to show him how much I actually liked this, but my nipples were hard, waiting for him to touch them.

I tugged off my shorts and handed them to him, sitting almost naked in his car. He laid my clothes on his lap, rubbed my pussy through my underwear, and played with one of my tits with his other hand. His mouth was on my neck, his scent drifting through my nose, his fingers moving so lightly against the fabric and making me so damn wet for him.

After sighing, I relaxed against the seat and spread my legs wider, giving him better access. Well, at least we were staying in the car. Melissa wouldn't come out here for anything unless she decided to leave, and it was too late for—

Michael's lips brushed against my ear. "Get out of the car," he said. "I want to eat this tight little cunt."

He opened his car door, grabbed my clothes, and walked right out of the car. I stared at him through the window with wide eyes.

From the sidewalk leading to his front door, he cocked his finger at me and mouthed the word, *Come*.

My heart pounded against my chest, and I glanced toward the backyard. Melissa could walk around the corner at any minute and see me completely naked in her front yard. I gulped, hurried out of the car, and shut the door softly behind me, so Melissa wouldn't be suspicious.

I held my forearm against my breasts, embarrassed that we were outside in the open—it wasn't like anyone could see us but still—and hurried to the front door. Michael pushed his key into the lock but didn't turn it.

"Put your arms down, Mia. I want to see you."

I stared up at his lustful eyes and clenched. I dropped my hands to my sides and watched him take my whole body in under the front light. He turned the key and pushed the door open for me.

After I took a deep breath, I hurried inside the house and up the stairs, trying to put as much space as possible between me and the pool. But Michael caught my wrist on the last stair and pulled me toward the living room.

"We're not going to my bedroom," he said.

I shook my head. "No, Michael, we can't! What if they come upstairs and—"

He pushed me down on the couch, knelt, and held my legs apart, staring down at my wet panties. He danced his fingers down my inner thighs, and I shivered from his touch. In one swoop, he hooked his finger inside of my underwear and pushed them to the side, placing his hot, wet mouth right on my pussy.

I threw my head back. Melissa's voice still drifted through the room through an open window, but I could barely make out what she was saying because her father was eating my pussy so fucking well that I couldn't even think straight.

"Play with your tits, Mia."

I groped my breasts and tugged on my nipples, letting out a quiet moan. He pushed two fingers inside of me and curled them, hitting my G-spot. My body jerked into the air, my breasts bouncing. He watched them and did it again, lips tugging into a smirk against me.

"Michael," I breathed out.

He pulled his fingers out of me and stuck them right in my mouth, pushing them as far down as they would go. I sucked on them and closed my eyes, my pussy aching to be filled by him. His tongue moved faster around my clit, and delight surged through me.

"Fuck, Mia," Michael groaned against me. "You're making me so hard."

I clenched again, heat warming me.

"Keep sucking on my fingers, baby."

He grunted against my folds, then kissed his way up my body to my breasts. His free hand started rubbing my clit until I was moments away from coming.

The sliding glass door opened downstairs, and I listened to Melissa's and Victor's footsteps. I sank down on the couch, glad that Michael had decided to keep the light off, and shook my head at him, telling him that we needed to stop. Now.

Instead of letting me go, he pushed his fingers deeper into my mouth and bit down on my nipple, tugging on it with his lips. My legs trembled, and I moved my hips from side to side, trying to displace all the ecstacy rushing right to my core because it was too much. I moaned loudly on his hand and squeezed my eyes closed, trying to be quiet.

But wave after wave of pleasure pumped through me, and my whole body felt like it was tingling. My torso jerked back and forth on the couch as I tried to breathe evenly.

"Oh, come on. Don't be such a pussy," Melissa said from downstairs.

I stared at Michael, my pussy pulsing over and over. He pulled his fingers out of my mouth and stood up, his swollen cock pressing against the front of his pants.

"Michael," I whispered, aching for him to fill me. "We can't."

Victor grumbled downstairs and said something incoherent, and Melissa laughed.

"Stop it. We've been fucking around for months. Now that you two are over, we can finally be together, *Mason*."

And my heart stopped.

CHAPTER 31

MIA

All I felt was anger, rage, and intense pain. I froze and stared up at Michael, whose sultry expression dropped and was replaced with a tense and confused one. Melissa continued laughing downstairs, and I didn't want to believe what she had said. She was my best friend.

But then I heard Mason saying the same things to her that he used to say to me when we first started dating. And I snapped. I hopped off the couch, snatched my shirt from Michael's hand, and pulled it over my head.

Before I could even stop myself to think about this rationally, I stormed down the stairs with Michael close behind me. Mason was lying on his back on the couch with Melissa straddling his waist, his hands slipping under her shirt and his gaze fixed on her tits.

"What the fuck are you doing?!" I screamed.

They both jumped up in surprise and looked in my direction.

Melissa pushed Mason away, lips parting and pressing together, as if she didn't know what to say.

I rushed toward them. "You two have been fucking behind my back for months?!" I shouted at them, and then I turned toward Melissa. "He was my fucking boyfriend, and you were supposed to be my best friend."

She shook her head. "Mia ... you always complained about him, and I—"

"So?!" I screamed, tears threatening to fall. "You were supposed to support me, not fuck him! Why would you do that to me?"

Mason stood and grabbed my arm. "Mia, settle down. It wasn't serious."

I ripped my arm out of his grip and glared at him. "Don't tell me to settle down," I said, my cheeks flushing. I stepped toward him and slammed my hands right into his chest. "You cheated on me for months. If you wanted to break up, you should've done it!"

I stepped toward him again, but Michael wrapped his arm around my waist and held me back.

His body was tense behind me, and I didn't have to turn around to know that he was as angry as I was. I could feel it. He pushed me behind him, his back muscles flexing through his shirt.

Melissa furrowed her brows. "Wait, why are you here and ..." She looked down at my bare legs. "Why don't you have pants on?"

My blood was boiling, and I didn't feel bad anymore for sleeping with her father. I crossed my arms over my chest and glared at her. "I'm here because I'm fucking your dad. And I don't give a single fuck about what you think about it anymore." Because she wasn't my friend.

"This is the guy you were fucking when you broke up with me?" Mason said. His jaw twitched, and he lunged toward Michael.

My heart pounded in my chest. I knew that Mason was a loose cannon. I didn't know what he'd do to Michael, so I stepped in front of Michael because I wanted to protect him, but Mason pushed me out of the way like I was nothing. I slammed into the wall, my head bouncing off it, and watched Mason swing at Michael. All I wanted to do was scream at him to stop, but I couldn't get myself to do it without choking on my tears.

Michael's eyes flickered to me, and he swiftly dodged Mason's stupid fucking punch, wrapped his hand around the front of his throat, and pulled him close. "Don't you dare put your hands on Mia or my daughter again."

Mason struggled in his hold, trying so desperately to get out, but Michael shoved him against the wall and leaned closer to him. His jaw was clenched, the vein in his neck prominent. He squeezed his hands hard until Mason was gasping for breath and clawing at his wrist. He said something into Mason's ear, so quietly that I couldn't hear it.

"Are you serious, Mia?" Melissa asked, drawing my attention away from Michael.

I cradled my head, pain shooting through it, and glared at her.

"Sleeping with my dad?! You want to talk about betrayal? *That* is betrayal."

I turned back toward her with hot, angry tears in my eyes. Why was she acting this way all of a sudden? Where had the last eighteen years of friendship gone? Why would she try to twist this on me? Sure, it was wrong to sleep with her father. But sleeping with my boyfriend for far longer was so much worse.

"Don't turn this back around on me," I said.

Mason had done that so many times before.

I glanced at Michael, who pushed Mason away from him. His muscles were flexed, a sinister expression written all over his face. Michael didn't lose his temper often. Hell, I'd never seen him even yell at Melissa before. But he looked ready to kill.

Mason stared at me, growled under his breath, and stomped

out the front door, making sure to slam it behind him like the child he was. I stared at the door with tears in my eyes, so overcome with emotions that I'd never thought I'd feel. Something deep down inside of me always knew Mason was a cheater, but I didn't think my best friend would be the one to sleep with him.

I'd trusted her more than anything. We had been friends our entire lives. Why would she betray me like this? Mason wasn't even that good in bed, he was a shit person, and he didn't care. Didn't she know that he'd treat her the same way after they got comfortable?

After Mason walked down the street to his parked car–which I should've freaking noticed before–and drove away, I crossed my arms over my chest.

Michael glared at Melissa, his jaw twitching. "Mia, take my keys and leave. I need to talk to my daughter." His voice was tenser than I had ever heard it, full of hurt and anger. And that look in his eyes told me that he was going to do more than *talk* to her. He would scold her.

I glanced at Michael, then at Melissa, who glared at *me* like I was in the wrong. And then I turned on my heel to walk up the stairs to the foyer.

Michael caught my arm before I left. "Keep your phone with you. Make sure Mason isn't following you."

My lips trembled, and I nodded. I grabbed the keys from the foyer and hurried out of the house. I promised myself I wouldn't cry in front of them. But as soon as I slid behind the wheel, started the car, and drove down the driveway, the tears flowed from my eyes.

CHAPTER 32

MICHAEL

When Mia left, Melissa snatched her keys from the coffee table and stormed past me. I grabbed them from her and shoved them into my pocket.

"You're not going anywhere," I said through gritted teeth, the anger bubbling inside of me.

Since I'd heard her say Mason's name, I had been holding myself back from snapping. I didn't want any trouble in front of Mia or for Mason to hurt her. She was too stressed already, but I would deal with Mason later. Melissa, on the other hand … I couldn't tell her to leave without punishing her for what she'd done.

"Give me my keys back," Melissa said, glaring at me with her mother's angry eyes.

All I felt was pure anger for letting her get this way. She reached for my pocket, but I stepped away.

"They're mine."

"I bought you the fucking car, Melissa. They aren't yours. Now, sit down."

After huffing to herself, she stomped over to the couch and sat down on it, crossing her arms over her chest. "How about we start with how you're fucking my best friend?"

"Your best friend?" I asked, stunned. "If you were friends with Mia, you wouldn't have been fucking Mason behind her back, and you wouldn't have pressured her into sleeping with Victor at a party."

Melissa suddenly got quiet for a moment. "I didn't pressure her into sleeping with him. We have threesomes all the time. I didn't see the problem, especially because she complains about Mason every single moment that I'm with her."

"The problem is, she called me to come get her because she didn't think she was safe. She called me because you couldn't be a good friend to her and watch her when you knew her mother was in the hospital. You wanted her to go to the party, and you fucking ditched her!" I slammed my palm against the wall and tried so desperately to hold myself together. After taking another deep breath, I said, "The problem is, you've been sleeping with her boyfriend for months." I shook my head, feeling so betrayed *for* Mia. "I thought I'd raised you better than that."

She glared at me without saying a word. "You don't have any room to talk. How long have you been sleeping with Mia? Was it while they were dating?"

My jaw twitched, my heart pounding against my chest. Melissa was acting like her mother. Going behind her boyfriend's back and betraying her closest friends to fuck someone who didn't know the first thing about sex. She was exactly like her, but I couldn't tell her that. So, instead, I pursed my lips.

"We've been seeing each other for a couple months, serious for only a couple weeks." I clenched my jaw. "How long have you known that Mason was treating Mia like shit and you let it happen?" I asked her, anger boiling inside of me again. "How long did you take advantage of your friendship to sleep with her boyfriend?"

"That's different," she said. "I love Mason."

My eyes widened. "You love Mason? Are you serious, Melissa?" I shook my head. "You're not seeing Mason. I will not allow it. He will do the same thing to you that he did to Mia. He will cheat on you time and time again."

"No, he won't," she said, standing up and crossing her arms over her chest. "He loves me. You know nothing about us."

"I was you," I shouted at her. "I let your mother cheat so we could stay a family *for you*. I believed that she loved me, but she betrayed me over and over. Don't fall for his lies or his stupid fucking games, Melissa. You're smarter than that."

My phone buzzed in my pocket, and I pulled it out to make sure Mia was okay. But instead of seeing her name on the screen, I saw Melissa's mother's name, and I shut the damn thing off. Why'd she always call at the worst times? All I wanted was for her to leave me the fuck alone. I shoved the phone back into my pocket and glanced up at Melissa.

"Is that your girlfriend?" she asked. "Mia, who you'll probably love more than you ever loved me?"

I closed my eyes and sighed through my nose. It broke my heart, hearing those words come out of her mouth because she knew that I did everything for her and that I would do anything for her. I had given her everything she could ever want for the past twenty-two years, and now, I was paying for it.

Was I a fool to let her take advantage of me? Was I a fool to let this happen to me again? Yes, and yes.

But she was my only daughter, and I wanted to give her the world. But she needed to be punished for this. I couldn't let her get away with it so easily.

"Until you learn respect, you can't stay here anymore. No more coming to use the pool. No more asking me for money. I'm done with paying your rent or any of your other bills. I'm sick of it."

"Are you serious?! How am I supposed to afford my apartment?"

"Get a job. Work hard. Learn respect."

"Dad, you can't do that to me. Not after what you did with my best friend."

"My relationship with Mia has nothing to do with this, so don't bring that into this argument. When you're really ready to talk about Mia and me, we can talk, but for now, I want you out."

When I didn't back down from her menacing glare, Melissa stomped upstairs, packed a bag of her stuff, snatched her keys back from me, and hauled it to her car. Without saying good-bye to me, she slammed her car door and sped down the road. I watched her tail lights disappear and frowned out the front door. Something about it was unsettling.

We had never fought before, especially like this. And I hated seeing her so angry, but she needed to learn a lesson. I couldn't have Melissa turn into her mother—a drunk who attempted to hurt whoever she could, whenever she could.

But what was worse than the thought of Melissa's mother was that my and Mia's secret was out … in the hands of my furious daughter and the man who I knew could ruin Mia's life. And I needed to make sure she wasn't in harm's way. Mia had been through too much these past few weeks. I wouldn't let Mason make it worse.

* * *

I WENT to the only place I thought Mia would go—the hospital to see her mother. Since visiting hours were almost over, it was quiet on the inside. The elevator was empty, and so was the waiting room. A few nurses passed me and nodded their heads as

I headed straight for Mia's mother's room. If Mia wasn't passed out in the waiting room, she'd be with her mother.

After I peered into the window and saw Mia's mother lying there alone, I frowned. Though the room was dim, I saw her look right over at me and smile. She motioned for me to come into the room, and I hesitated. What was I going to say to her? That I'd lost her daughter and it hadn't even been an hour since we'd left her?

"Michael, did you leave something here?" she asked, her voice frail.

I shut the door behind me and shook my head. "I'm looking for Mia."

She furrowed her brows. "Mia? Didn't she leave with you?"

Again, I hesitated. *Well, here goes nothing. What a great start to our relationship, great impression on her mother too.* I took a deep breath. "Yes, but ..." Did I tell her about what had happened between Mason and my daughter? She was going to ask about why I'd told Mia to leave the house. "I took her back to my home to ..."

God, I hadn't stumbled over my words like this in years.

She smiled gently and pushed herself up to a sitting position. "To?"

"I took your daughter home because I care about her," I said, swallowing my pride and telling her straight up that I had feelings for her daughter. I didn't play games anymore. I wanted to be with Mia, and I wanted to be with her bad. "I wanted her to rest, but she and my daughter got into a fight, so I asked her to leave."

"You asked my daughter to leave? What happened to caring about her?"

The words hurt, and I realized that they had come out different than I'd intended them to. "I asked her to leave, so I could discipline my daughter for—"

"Does Melissa know about you and Mia?" she asked, interrupting me. "Is that why they got into a fight?"

I felt so much guilt for Melissa's actions. I couldn't believe my own daughter would do something like that to her best friend after what her mother had done to us. It didn't make sense to me, but I couldn't hide my daughter's mistakes. She had to own up to them.

"Yes, she knows. But they got into a fight for a different reason," I said, shaking my head.

Eden glanced down at her lap and gulped. "Did Mason cheat on her?" she asked suddenly, as if she already knew but wanted confirmation.

I paused for a long moment and stuffed my hands into my pockets. "It's not really my place to tell you about it. I'd rather you talk to Mia." There was only so much I could say about it. I couldn't speak on what Mia had gone through. Hell, I doubted she wanted to live through Mason's torture again.

She sighed to herself and closed her eyes, a tear falling from her cheek. "My daughter deserves so much better than him." When she reopened her eyes, she stared directly at me and wiped the tear with the back of her hand. "I don't love the age gap between you and her, but I need her to be happy. Are you going to make her happy, or is this some fling? Because if it is, I'm going to kindly ask you to stop it right now before she gets hurt."

"This isn't a fling," I said, pulling a chair next to her bed and sitting down in it. "I would do anything to see her happy. I told her from day one that she deserves someone better than Mason."

After a few moments of silence, she nodded. "Good, because …" She grabbed my hand and squeezed. "I need to be honest with you …" There was a long pause, and I held my breath, unsure if I'd like this honesty right now. She sounded too weak and too sad for it to be anything good. She frowned. "I don't know if I'll survive this round of surgery."

My gaze fell to the bed. I didn't know what to say, and I didn't know what I'd say to Mia if something happened to her mother.

Mia's mother grabbed my chin and made me look back up at her. "Oh, don't do that. I need you to be strong and to take care of my daughter because I know that I never will. I've been getting weaker and weaker. I've been trying to be optimistic around Mia, but … it's difficult for me to do the simplest things anymore. If this surgery doesn't kill me—"

"Don't say that," I said, shaking my head. "You're going to survive. And when you do, I'll send you and Mia on a relaxing vacation somewhere." It was what they needed after all of this.

She smiled up at me. "Don't get your hopes up. I'm being honest with you." Her voice was quiet. "Save your money and take Mia somewhere nice. Make her happy. She deserves it after what her father and then Mason put her through. I can tell she's worn out, but you make her happier than I've ever seen her. She has that spark in her eyes again."

I opened my mouth to speak, to deny that she would die during surgery, but she shook her head.

"Please don't argue with me. I don't have the strength for it. All I ask is that you take care of her. She needs to be loved by a man. All she knows is hurt and betrayal."

After a couple of moments, I nodded at her. I didn't believe that she'd die. I didn't *want* to believe it, but she was asking for me to love her daughter … something I already did.

"And, Michael, please don't tell her we had this chat. I don't want her to worry."

CHAPTER 33

MIA

I didn't have anywhere to go. I couldn't go back to the hospital because I knew Mason would be waiting for me in the parking lot, looking for a fight. I couldn't stay at Michael's because I knew he and Melissa were about to get into the fight of the decade. So, I went to the one place I knew I'd be somewhat safe.

Serena's apartment.

When I parked in front of the townhouse, I had stopped crying, but my eyes were bloodshot, my whole body hurt, and I just wanted someone to make me smile. The light turned on in her front window, and she peeked her head out from behind the curtain to see me.

A few moments later, she appeared at Michael's passenger door. "Why do you have his—what's wrong?" she asked, brows immediately furrowing.

I stormed out of the car, slammed the car door shut, and pulled her into a tight hug, resting my head on her shoulder. I didn't know what to say, but Serena was the only person who seemed to accept this thing going on between Michael and me.

She cradled me for a moment, and then she pulled away and tugged me toward the family-owned ice cream shop around the corner called Sprinkling. "Tell me what happened over ice cream. That always makes things better."

We walked toward Sprinkling, which was known for the sheer number of sprinkles that they smothered on all their ice cream.

After ordering, I slumped onto one of the wooden benches and licked some of the rainbow sprinkles off my vanilla ice cream. "Melissa knows about me and Michael," I said to break the silence. I didn't know if that was a good starting place to talk about the shit I had witnessed, but that was the only thing I could get myself to say.

Serena's eyes widened. "She does? How'd she find out? What'd she say?"

My lips quivered, and I bit the damn ice cream, so I'd get brain-freeze instead of crying again. My two front teeth stung, and I leaned forward. "She was at the house when Michael and I came home. And she—"

Serena plastered a big smile on her face. "Did she see you two fucking?"

"No," I said. "I actually caught her with Mason."

Serena's face went totally blank, and her cone almost slipped out of her hand. She choked on her ice cream, shook her head, and gave me the most confused expression of the damn century. "What'd you just say? She was with Mason?"

"Turns out, she's been sleeping with him for months."

She balled her hand into a fist, and her cone broke to pieces in her hand, the ice cream going everywhere. "Are you fucking serious?! She was fucking Mason, out of all fucking people." She shook her head, a solemn expression crossing her face. "I … I … I'm sorry, Mia."

But she had nothing to apologize for. It wasn't her fault that our best friend was a no-good, betraying bitch who fucked people's boyfriends and didn't seem to have a problem with it. I bit my ice cream again, but this time, I was angry. I couldn't believe she'd done this to me. Why would she hurt me like that? Did all our years of friendship mean nothing to her?

"I don't know what to say," Serena said, scooting closer to me and pulling me into a tight hug. "I'm so sorry she did this to you. You don't deserve that. I'm so disappointed in her."

I rested my head on her shoulder and stared at the wooden bench. At this point, I felt numb to all this pain. It was heartbreak after heartbreak, and I just wanted to spend some quality time with Michael. We didn't even have to fuck. We could have some wine and stay up late and make waffles at three in the morning. I didn't care.

"When I see her, I'm going to—"

"It's fine," I said to Serena. "Michael is taking care of her ..." I hoped.

After we finished our ice cream, we walked back to the apartment. Damien's sister was walking out of the house with her newborn, cradling her in her arms.

"Hey, girls," she said to us, eyes flickering to me. "You want to see Anna?"

Damien's sister handed Anna to Serena. Serena smiled at the baby, giving her a kiss on her nose. I smiled and gazed lovingly at her. Her skin was so soft, and she was dressed in a pink onesie. Something so pure in this fucked-up world. Serena handed her to me despite my death stare telling her not to, and I cradled Anna's head in the crook of my arm.

"Does Daddy Bryne want another kid?" Serena asked.

I almost choked on the air. I handed the baby back to her mother and narrowed my eyes at Serena. "Quiet down," I said, glancing up at her open apartment window. "Just because Mason and Melissa know doesn't mean I need the entire world knowing yet."

Serena said good-bye to Damien's sister and rocked back on her heels. "That didn't answer my question."

"Serena, I have so much going on right now. I haven't even told him that I love—" I stopped mid-sentence. I hadn't said it out loud yet, and I really hadn't admitted it to anyone else except Mom.

"You love him," she said. She pulled me into a hug and rested her head on my shoulder. Her vanilla scent was oddly comforting. "Mia, I am so happy for you. After everything you've been through, you've finally found someone who really makes you happy and treats you right."

After walking to her apartment, I spotted Victor lying back on Serena's couch, playing video games with Damien, and sighed. The last time I had seen him, he had been drunk in bed at the party. Yet he didn't look at me any different for running out of the room or after listening to Mason label me as a whore to every single one of our friends.

When Serena saw Victor, she narrowed her eyes. "Did you know?"

Damien stared between all three of us and put his video game controller down on the coffee table. "What's going on?" he asked her, brows furrowed together, noticing Serena's death glare.

Victor glanced up at us, realized Serena was staring directly at him, and blew out a deep breath, tossing his controller onto the couch. "Did I know what?"

"About Melissa and Mason."

Victor narrowed his eyes, then looked at me. "What about them?"

"They've been sleeping together for months," Serena said. "Mia found them together."

"What the fuck did you say?" Victor said, jaw clenching, hands balled into tight fists. He glanced at me, waiting for me to confirm or deny it. "Are you serious, Mia?"

I nodded, but part of me didn't think he'd believe me. He and Mason had been best friends for such a long time, similar to Melissa and me. I didn't know if he'd believe what the so-called *whore* had to say about his relationship. But Victor deserved to know either way.

"Yes, they admitted to it."

"They've been fucking?" He marched past us to the front door and slammed it open. "Why would I fucking know that?"

I shrugged my shoulders. "You were okay with having threesomes with her. I thought maybe you knew about it."

"Threesomes, not cheating," he said through gritted teeth. His whole body was tense, and he was visibly shaking. He walked down the stairs toward his car. "Where is that fucker now? I'm going to go kick his ass."

Serena grabbed my hand and followed him. "Come on."

I dug my heels into the ground. "I am not going to see Mason."

"Girl, we're going to go get your stuff from his apartment and enjoy the beatdown of his sorry ass. You aren't going to talk to him one time."

So, we all piled into Victor's car, and Victor drove like a maniac to Mason's apartment. The whole time, my heart was pounding against my chest, my jaw was twitching, and my legs were bouncing. I hadn't seen Mason for a long time. I needed my stuff, but I didn't know if I needed it this badly. I could wait until I was with Michael, or I could wash my clothes I already had at the hospital.

Serena placed her hand on my knee and squeezed. "Settle down. Everything will be okay. If Mason tries to hurt you, Damien will kick his ass." She leaned closer. "And we can always call Daddy Bryne to take care of this mess."

Instead of rolling my eyes, I let out a small laugh. I didn't know what had made me do it, but something about the mention of Michael made me not feel as scared. All I wanted to do was tell him already that I loved him, but I hadn't found the right time. It all still felt too soon, and I didn't want to be the first one to say it because I didn't know if he felt the same way yet.

Victor skirted around the bend and found the first parking spot he could in front of Mason's apartment building. He stormed out of the car, his hands balled into fists and his eyes trained on the entrance door in front of him. I punched the code into it to gain access to the building like I had for the last five years.

Serena looped her arm around mine. "I cannot wait to see his ass get dropped."

We piled into the elevator, and Victor hit the button for floor six. My heart pounded in my chest with every floor we went up, and I swallowed nervously. I wanted to get my stuff and get out of there.

"I don't want him to hurt me," I whispered.

Damien looked down at me and nodded. "He won't touch you."

"The only damn person getting his ass beat is Mason," Victor said, voice laced with anger.

As soon as the elevator doors opened, Victor hurried out of them and walked directly toward Mason's apartment. He banged on his door with the side of his fist. "Mason, it's Victor. Open the fucking door."

He knocked two more times, and I waited so damn anxiously out of sight.

Suddenly, the door opened, and Mason stood before us with a towel wrapped around his waist and beads of water running down his chest. "Dude, wha—"

Victor swung right at his face, hitting him square in the jaw.

Serena intertwined our fingers together and pulled me toward the back bedroom, letting out a, "*Woohoo*."

She slammed the door closed and grabbed one of Mason's

luxury suitcases from the closet, opened all my drawers, and threw all my clothes inside of it. "Get whatever's yours. We're not leaving until you have everything back."

I opened all the drawers and closets and went through all of Mason's things to find whatever he had of mine. All my clothes, all my jewelry, all the cute little presents I had made for his birthday that he kept in a box in the back of his closet. He didn't deserve them. He didn't deserve anything that I had gotten him.

It took a swift five minutes to pack everything into one small suitcase, but we did it, and I couldn't have felt more ... free. It felt like another weight had been lifted off my shoulders, and I didn't have to worry at all about Mason anymore because we were over for good.

Serena lifted the suitcase and handed it to Damien, who stood outside the door. "How's he looking out there?" Serena asked him.

Damien stared down the hall and smirked. "See for yourself."

We peered out the hallway to see Mason pinned against the wall by Victor. Both of his eyes were black already ... and I laughed. It was terrible of me to do, but it happened, and I couldn't stop myself. All of the tears I'd had for that man turned into a fit of giggles.

Mason tried so desperately to squirm out of his hold but couldn't. Just like he couldn't with Michael earlier. He was all talk, no walk. I clutched my stomach and rested my forehead on Serena's, trying hard to breathe between giggles.

"You fucked my girlfriend?" Victor said between gritted teeth. "For fucking months?!"

"Mia fucked her father," Mason said.

Victor didn't let the words even faze him. "I don't give a fuck what she did. You fucked *my* girlfriend." He landed another punch straight on the damn smirk on his face. "You're more fucked up than I thought."

He pushed Mason away. Mason stumbled, then tripped on the

table beside him, his towel falling off and exposing all his family *jewels.*

Serena scrunched her nose and stared at Mason's nakedness. "And you wonder why you couldn't keep Mia," she said, looking him up and down in disgust.

She grabbed my hand, pulled me to the front door, and pushed me out of it. "You're done with his no-good, tiny-dick, womanizing ass."

CHAPTER 34

MIA

Victor wrapped his hand tightly around the steering wheel, his knuckles covered in Mason's blood. I stared out the windshield, feeling so good. My suitcase was in the back, Serena was smiling widely at me, and I was finally free of that idiot. It felt like nothing could stop me.

Until I saw Melissa's car parked in front of Serena's.

She stood outside her car, arms crossed over her chest. Victor swore under his breath and parked the car behind hers. He took unsteady breaths and balled and unballed his hands. I sat behind him, staring wide-eyed over his shoulder.

What the hell is she doing here?

Serena grabbed my hand. "Let me handle this. Don't get out of the car." She unbuckled her seat belt and slid out of the car with Damien, walking straight toward her.

After a few softly spoken words between them, Melissa started to freak out. Throwing her hands into the air. Pointing her fingers at Victor's car. Screaming so loud that the entire neighborhood probably heard her.

Victor hit the steering wheel. "I can't handle this shit," he said, hopping out of the car and jumping in on the fight.

All I could hear was her screaming at him and him shouting at her, asking her why she hadn't been faithful.

And that was when I got out of the car because it was damn hot in there and I felt like I was suffocating.

"Is that why you wanted me to have sex with Mia?" Victor asked, hurt laced in his voice. "You wanted to make yourself feel better about what you were doing?"

"I am not talking to you about this," Melissa said, jaw twitching, turning toward Serena.

Victor snatched her wrist and pulled her back. "When are you going to start taking responsibility for your actions?" he asked. "Just admit that you fucked him. Admit that you went behind my back, *Mia's* back, our whole friend group's back to fuck Mason."

She stared at me with tears in her eyes. Just by looking at her, I could feel how hurt she was, and it made me hurt even worse. I wrapped my arms around my body. I had fucked up too. It wasn't solely her fault. I had slept with her father and hidden it from her for over a month. If she had slept with mine... I'd feel the same way.

But that didn't erase my pain of knowing that she'd slept with Mason even though she knew how terrible he was to me. I complained about him so damn much, and she didn't think twice about hooking up with him. She'd even wanted me to sleep with Victor—her boyfriend—probably so she wouldn't feel as bad about it.

The empath in me wanted to apologize to her for sleeping with her father, but it didn't even seem like she was remorseful at all for what she had done with Mason. She continued to stare at me with tears in her eyes, giving me that expression that told me *I* was the only one in the wrong.

Victor growled, "We are done, Melissa. I don't want to hear from you ever again. Don't come crawling back to me when Mason sleeps with woman after woman at frat parties and won't let you look at another man without getting jealous."

And if that didn't sum up Mason's abuse in a sentence, I didn't know what could.

Melissa clenched her jaw and shook her head. "It's not like that, Victor. You can't—" Tears started streaming from her face. "Please, I don't have anywhere to go. Let me stay with you tonight."

She doesn't have anywhere to go? Has Michael kicked her out of the house?

Victor shook his head. "That's not my problem. I'm not the one who slept with someone else. You should've thought about what you were doing before you did it."

"Let me get the stuff from our apartment," she said so desperately.

"No," Victor said. "You can get it while I'm at work tomorrow. Go stay at Mason's tonight. He's going to need all the fucking love tonight after what I did to him."

Melissa glanced down at his bloody knuckles, her face contorting into even more pain. "Did you hurt him?"

Victor looked upset, betrayed, and so fucking sad. He shook his head, pulled my suitcase out of the trunk of the car, and slid into the driver's seat. "I'm done, Melissa. I can't handle this anymore. It fucking hurts." And then he sped off into the night, his tail lights disappearing down the street.

Melissa looked back at me. "Why'd you do it?" she asked quietly, shaking her head. "Why'd you do that to me? He's my dad." She sounded so heartbroken.

I furrowed my brows and frowned at her, not having any words. Why did I sleep with her dad, or why did I love him? Those were two different answers, and I didn't think she was ready for either of them.

Serena pressed her lips together. "You should leave, Melissa."

Melissa grumbled under her breath and got into her car. She slammed her car door and sped down the road, toward Mason's apartment.

I frowned at her car, threw my head back, and let out the loudest, "Ugh," of my entire life.

To say that I felt guilt wasn't even enough to explain how I felt at this moment. I felt guilty, betrayed, like a shitty person. Every single negative emotion that I could ever have was bundled into a one-hundred-thirty-five-pound struggling college student trying to get her shit together but failing miserably.

"Don't listen to her," Serena said, wrapping one arm around me and grabbing my suitcase with the other. She pulled me toward Michael's car and pushed the suitcase into the backseat. "You didn't do anything wrong."

"Yes, I did," I whispered. "Sleeping with her father was wrong."

Serena frowned at me and paused. "Well, I'm here for you," she said. "You can stay the night here or go back to Mr. Bryne's, but … I want to make sure you know that Damien and I"—she glanced over at Damien, who stood with his hands on his hips a few feet away—"we don't think of you any differently. You're going through a lot right now, and Mason wasn't good for you. Ever."

I gulped and nodded. "I know."

"Now, you want to watch scary movies all night, or are you going to go sleep with Mr. Bryne?"

My phone buzzed in my pocket, and I pulled it out to read Michael's name. Serena smiled widely at me and pushed me toward the car.

"We'll see you early Friday morning at the hospital for your mom's surgery," she said. "If you need anything before then, text me."

CHAPTER 35

MIA

Michael waited for me at his front door, leaning against the frame with his arms crossed over his chest and an unreadable expression on his face. I left my suitcase in the trunk because I didn't want to intrude on him in case he didn't want me to stay here yet. I handed him the keys and pushed my lips to his, needing this.

"Where'd you go?" he asked, closing the door behind us.

"Serena's house, and then I got my stuff from Mason's." I walked up the stairs toward his bedroom, wanting to rest.

Michael grasped my hips from behind before I could reach the room and held me against him. "You went to Mason's? Did he say anything to you? You'd better have gone with someone."

I turned around in his embrace and brushed my thumb over his taut jaw. "Victor, Damien, and Serena. Mason didn't even talk to me. He was too occupied with Victor."

"And your stuff?" Michael asked, brow raised. "Where is it?"

"In the trunk."

"Why didn't you bring it in?"

My cheeks flushed, and I stared down at my feet, wiggling my toes in my sandals. I shrugged my shoulders, feeling so damn weird about barging in with all my belongings. It wasn't like I had much, but still.

He paused for a few moments, grabbed my chin, and forced me to look up at him. There were so many emotions pooling in his eyes, and I thought that he would scold me for it because that was what Mason and Dad always did when I did something wrong. But Michael pulled me closer and pressed his lips to mine.

In one heated moment, he lifted me off the ground and shoved me against the wall. I kissed him back, tangling my hands into his hair and tugging on it gently. I wrapped my legs around his waist and pulled him closer to me.

From my shoulders to my breasts to my hips, his hands were all over my body. He grabbed my ass to hold me up and walked with me to his bedroom. When he kicked his bedroom door closed, he let me down and pushed me back onto his bed. Everything about him felt like it did every other night, but tonight, something also felt different.

I tugged on the ends of his hair, pulling him to me. He kissed me, matching my intensity. Butterflies fluttered around in my stomach, and all I wanted him to do tonight was love me.

Not fuck me. Not take me so roughly.

Love me.

He slipped his fingers into my underwear, rubbing me and making me wet with delight. I moaned against his lips, and then as his lips traveled down the column of my neck, I arched my back. He slipped two fingers inside of me and groaned. I smiled against his lips, clenching on his fingers, the feeling sending pleasure through me.

He rested his forehead against mine and pumped his fingers in and out of me so slowly that it started to drive me insane. I unbuttoned his belt and pulled it off of him, and then I wrapped my legs around his body to pull him toward me, feeling his dick against my pussy. I pushed his pants down with my feet and took his cock in my hand, stroking his hardness as he fingered me.

"I want you inside of me, Michael," I whispered against his lips.

He pressed his lips to mine, then peppered kisses down my body. He pulled my shirt up my body and tugged it over my head, then latched on to one of my nipples with his teeth, biting down. I moaned and pushed my breasts closer to him. He groped the other one, and then his lips moved from one to the other, his gray eyes gazing up at me.

After a few moments of sucking gently, his mouth traveled down my stomach until he reached my core. He hooked two fingers under the hem of my panties, peeled them off of me, and set his hot mouth on me.

I loved every moment of us together, and I moved my pussy against his face. His tongue rubbed my clit in torturous little circles, and he stroked his cock. I pulled him back up to me, unable to hold off much longer. With my legs wrapped around his waist, he shoved his dick against my entrance.

"Please, Michael," I said as he pushed into me.

He smiled down and kissed me. Then, he thrust himself into me tenderly, filling me. Everything about him, all my feelings toward him, felt so utterly intense as he pushed into me.

I clenched around him. He pulled out, and I tightened again. He cursed under his breath and pushed himself back into me, making me moan.

"More, Michael."

He caressed my cheek, pulled himself out, then pushed himself back in—this time quicker. Every stroke drove me closer to the edge already. I dug my nails into his back. He continued to fuck me faster and rougher, leaving me begging for him to never stop. This feeling was more than I could have ever asked for. I never wanted it to end. I wanted to feel this good all the time.

My legs shook uncontrollably. I grabbed on to him, hoping he wouldn't stop, and he didn't.

"Come for me, Mia," he whispered in my ear.

I dug my nails into his back and screamed his name. He pumped into me once more, then stilled deep in my pussy. He stared down at me with so much love, and I peered up at him with so much more.

His fingers danced across my collarbone. He pulled out of me and crawled onto the bed next to me. He snaked his fingers in my hair and pulled me closer. A chill ran through my body, yet everything inside of me seemed to warm.

* * *

"WHAT'S WRONG? YOU SEEM OFF," he said after fifteen minutes of silence.

There was so much on my mind that I didn't even know where to start. First, there was Mom, and then there was Melissa. I felt so much guilt and betrayal and heartbreak, but I just wanted to be happy for the smallest moment.

"I'm nervous about my mom's surgery," I started.

Michael tensed quite suddenly and pulled me closer to him, so my head was resting against his shoulder.

"I'm scared she won't make it. She's the only family I have left."

She had been through almost a hundred surgeries since her first accident and had come out victorious each time, but I was always anxious every time. Anything could go wrong during surgery.

I took a deep breath. "And Melissa ... she has a right to be angry with me," I said quietly, drawing my finger against his bare chest. Moonlight streamed into the room from the window, and I sighed to myself. "I'm sleeping with her father, and that ... doesn't make me the best of friends either."

His chest rose and fell as he took a deep breath. "I'm not going to say that you're wrong, Mia, because it isn't right. But I don't regret it," he said.

I glanced up at him, watching his eyes dance under the moonlight. They were like the sky on a stormy day, light gray and full of angst.

And in that moment, I wanted to come out and tell him that I loved him because I truly did. Nobody had shown me so much respect and love before that it made me feel good on the inside. I interlocked my fingers with his and pressed my lips to his soft ones.

But instead of telling him that I loved him, I said, "I don't either," which was almost the same thing.

He smiled, but the smile didn't meet his eyes. He looked tired, exhausted, and defeated—which I had never seen before from him. There was so much on his mind that I hadn't asked him about, and I felt bad about it. I sat up, pulling the blankets with me, and brushed my fingers through his hair. He closed his eyes and relaxed under my touch.

"Are you okay?" I asked.

It was his own daughter, the one person he had spent the most time with ever. I knew how much he loved her, and I didn't want to drive a barrier between them. As much as I didn't like her right now, Melissa deserved to have someone in her life who cared about her. I didn't want her to end up like me—without a stable father figure in her life. Michael was so good for her.

He sighed through his nose and stared up at me. "Yeah, I'm fine."

"Michael, please don't tell me you're fine when you're not."

He paused and grabbed my hand, his thumb swept over my knuckles. "I don't want you to worry. I know that your mother's surgery is stressing you out. We can talk about it this weekend."

I trapped his thumb with my own, forcing him to stop. "Tell me now. It'll make me feel so much less useless, and I ... care about you. I want you to be okay with everything going on, and I don't want to step between you and Melissa."

After a couple moments of silence, his eyes searching mine, he said, "I care about you too." He wrapped his arms around me and buried his face into the crook of my neck. "We haven't fought like this," he said. "Melissa and I have always had a good relationship. I just ..."

"I'm sorry," I said. "I shouldn't have—"

"This fight would've happened with or without you, Mia, so don't think you caused this. Ever since she went to college, she's changed. She's become more and more like her mother. I needed to confront her, but I'd been pushing it off for years now. If I hadn't, maybe this wouldn't have happened."

"If you hadn't ... maybe *we* wouldn't have happened."

Michael tensed and gazed up at me. He parted his lips, then pressed them back together a few times, as if he wanted to say something but didn't know how to say it. He pushed a strand of hair behind my ear and pulled me onto his chest. "I talked to your mother about us."

I rested my palm on his taut chest, feeling the muscle underneath. "When?"

"When I went looking for you. I thought you'd be at the hospital."

"What did she say?"

"That she loves and cares about you and that she wants you to be with someone who does the same thing," he said, his voice quiet.

My heart leaped in my chest, and I didn't know if he meant what he'd said or if he even realized what he'd indirectly said.

Michael wasn't one to beat around the bush. If he meant something, he would come out and say it, no matter how difficult it would be for him to speak it or for the other person to take it.

So, part of me wanted to ignore the fact he had just indirectly said the L-word.

But the other part of me couldn't because I loved and cared about Michael the same way Mom always loved and cared about me—with my whole heart, no matter how rough it got.

CHAPTER 36

MICHAEL

On Friday morning, Mia and I were at the hospital at three-thirty a.m., an hour and a half before her mother's scheduled surgery. She couldn't sleep all last night, tossing and turning in my arms over and over again. And when she had told me about her fears with her mom the other night, I'd wanted to tell her what we had talked about, but I'd promised her mother that I wouldn't say a word.

Instead, I'd held her tightly and vowed that I'd take care of her, no matter what.

She kissed me on the lips in front of everyone here already—Serena, Victor, and Damien—and disappeared into the hallway to go be with her mother. I wanted to follow her because I knew she was hurting, but I let them have some bonding time for the hour or so they had left.

My stomach was in knots as I sat next to Serena and sipped on my coffee. I didn't think her mother would make it out alive. I wanted to think she would, but I couldn't. The way she'd sounded the other night ... it made me less optimistic than Mia.

The elevator doors opened, and I glanced up from the ground to see Melissa walk into the waiting room. I blew out a deep breath and stood up before she could cause any trouble.

I caught her wrist in my hand and pulled her into the hallway. "You shouldn't be here, Melissa. What are you doing?"

Melissa paused for a long moment, tears in her eyes. "I'm not here to talk to you. I'm here for Mia."

I glanced toward the direction of Mia's mother's room. "Do you think she wants to see you now? This might be the last time she sees her mother. She doesn't need this extra drama right now."

Melissa's eyes softened. "The doctors think she won't survive?" Her voice was gentle, and I could tell that this wasn't a front. She actually cared about Mia's mother, like her own. "Did they tell you that?"

"Don't tell Mia," I said quietly, hoping to God that she'd listen to me for once. But ... I didn't want to hide it from her.

Melissa used to escape my and her mother's constant fighting by going over to Mia's house all the time. Mia's mother was like a second mom to Melissa, and I couldn't have been more thankful. But it only made this hurt all that much worse.

"I talked with her mother the other night, and she doesn't think she's going to make it."

Melissa doubled over, burying her face into my chest and letting out a quiet sob. "No," she said to herself. "No, she has to." She shook her head. "God, I've been such a shitty friend to Mia. I didn't think that this was this serious. I-I-I should've paid more attention. I should've loved her more."

She wrapped her arms around me, and I hesitantly hugged her back.

I stood there, holding my daughter as her tears stained my shirt. "Listen to me," I said to Melissa. "If her mother doesn't survive this, Mia won't have anyone left. She doesn't have her father. She doesn't have Mason anymore. She was worried about losing you once you found out about us. You either need to talk to her when this is all over or not talk to her again. Acting how you did with her boyfriend and then turning this around on her was immature of you. We should've told you sooner, I agree, but Mia didn't want to for this reason. She knew you'd take it badly. She didn't want to hurt your friendship."

"But she did," she said. "I feel so betrayed."

"So does Mia," I said, "knowing that you slept with her boyfriend for months behind her back when she told you how terrible he was to her. We're all in the wrong, Melissa. You can't blame only her and me."

Melissa wiped some tears from her cheeks with the back of her hand. "I know. I just ... she never loved Mason, and Mason never loved her."

"That doesn't make it right, and it doesn't make it right that you tried to coerce her to sleep with Victor to make it even." I shook my head and stared down at my daughter.

She didn't say anything for a long time, just pressed her lips together and frowned at me.

"Now, please tell me that you're not dating that loser," I said, hoping that she understood her mistake. It had only been a day or so, but I had faith in her. "He's going to cheat on you."

Melissa grimaced. "I can't tell you that." She took a deep breath. "But I took your advice and applied for a couple jobs down in the city. They aren't what I'd prefer to do, but it's something." She glanced down at her feet. "I know I screwed up, but do you understand how I felt when I found out that *you* were sleeping with my best friend?"

I paused for a long moment. "I'm truly sorry for not thinking about you before I slept with her, but ..." I blew out a deep breath through my nose. I did feel bad about this whole thing. I hadn't heard from Melissa for a day or so, which was weird for me, and

I didn't like it. But she needed to know that Mia wasn't going to go away. "I'm serious about her."

"Dad," she said, quietly, "she's my age. How would you feel if I slept with her father?"

"I would feel like a shitty father," I admitted, a heap of guilt washing over me. If I were in her position, I'd be angry too. "But I also feel like a shitty father, knowing that you're with Mason. You deserve more than anything he could give you."

Melissa's frown deepened. "I guess that we won't see eye to eye on this." She crossed her arms over her chest. "If you're going to see Mia, I have the right to see whoever I want to see too."

I sighed deeply through my mouth. I didn't know how to get her to see that Mason was bad for her. Maybe she needed the heartbreak to understand what it felt like to value someone like Victor or her friends. I didn't know. But I would keep pushing her to see that Mason wasn't the one for her. She was an adult. She had to make this decision for herself.

"Sit down," I said, nodding toward the waiting room. "Mia should be out soon."

CHAPTER 37

MIA

I peered into Mom's room, my heart racing. She lay on her bed, smiling wide when she saw me. After taking a deep breath and promising that I'd do my best to hold myself together, I walked into the room and shut the door behind me.

Mom patted the bed next to her, and I lay down, wrapping my arms around her bony waist. She grasped my hand and stayed quiet for a few moments, enjoying this silence. Her hold was frail and not as strong as it used to be, and my heart broke.

"Mia, you know that I love you very much." Tears welled up in her eyes, and I frowned at her. "You're my only daughter, my sunshine. You have made me so proud and happy these past twenty-two years."

A tear rolled down my cheek. "And I'll make you happy for years to come," I said. "This surgery will go fine, and you're going to come out of it stronger than before. You will."

But as I said those words, it felt like I was only talking to myself, trying to make myself feel better because Mom didn't agree with me. She stared at me with glossy eyes and a heartbreaking smile that told me she didn't think so.

"Mia, you have to be strong for me. I want to be honest about this, but you make it so difficult because I don't want to see you cry." She wiped some tears from my cheeks. "I don't know if I'll survive this surgery. I don't feel as strong as I did the first time around."

"No," I whispered, my heart hurting. "Don't say that."

"Mia, it's true," she said.

I curled up next to her and rested my head on her shoulder, my body jerking back and forth as hiccups escaped my lips. I couldn't lose Mom. I couldn't. I loved her so much that it hurt. She was the only person I loved unconditionally. She had taught me so much. I held on to her, listening to the steady rhythm of her heart, and didn't know if this would be the last time I heard it.

She rested her cheek on my head and stroked my hair. "I love you so much, sweetheart, and I want you to know that whatever happens, I will always be with you."

"Mom," I choked out. "Please … don't say that." My whole heart was hurting.

"I need you to be strong, Mia. You are an amazing woman, and I want you to know that you can make your own decisions. Don't depend on someone. Don't let any man rule you. Don't let things go unchecked. I want you to be happy and healthy and to live without regrets."

"Mom, stop." Tears streamed down my cheeks and stained her hospital gown. I wanted to yell at her that she was going to survive this, but I didn't know if she would.

She took my face in her hands and forced me to look at her. And all I could do was cry even harder. "Promise me that you'll do that," she said to me. "I need you to promise me."

I shook my head, my chest heaving back and forth. "Mom, please, don't say this. I … I can't … I don't want to lose you. I love you so much." I placed a hand over my mouth to try to hold back my sobs, but I couldn't.

"Listen to me, Mia," Mom said, her voice stronger.

I couldn't resist looking into her eyes, which, while they looked so sad, were so damn strong.

"Promise me that you won't take any more abuse from a man; that you will finish school, no matter what happens; that you'll be happy in every aspect of your life because you can't live with regrets. I want you to succeed in life, in your career, in your family. Make a family and be happy. Visit me when I'm gone. Okay?"

I blinked, trying to push away the tears, but I couldn't. So, I nodded and bit my lip, holding back my hiccups. "I promise you." I took her face in my shaky hands. "I promise you."

Dr. Jackson knocked on the metal door and popped his head into the room. "It's time," he said to Mom. "Mia, I have to ask you to wait in the waiting room with your friends."

My lips quivered, and I pulled Mom closer to me and into a tight hug. She hugged me back, wrapping her arms around me and holding me so close because we didn't know if this was the last time we would ever see each other.

I held her for as long as I could, resting my head against hers and sobbing so loudly that everyone could hear me. "Mom, I love you with all my heart." Salty tears ran down my face.

"Mia," Dr. Jackson said again, resting his hand on my shoulder. "It's time to go."

But I didn't want to let go of Mom. I didn't want to never see her again. I loved her so fucking much, and something was telling me that this was the final time I'd ever see her like this. She was the only family I had left, the only person I could turn to who would love me unconditionally, the only person I loved like that.

"Mia," Dr. Jackson said.

Mom pulled away from me, eyes filled with tears. "I love you, sweetheart."

Dr. Jackson grabbed my arms lightly and pulled me to the door, yet I didn't take my eyes off of Mom the entire time. I didn't want to leave her. I couldn't leave her. I … I couldn't.

As soon as the door closed, I buckled over, unable to hold myself up. Everything hurt so fucking bad.

CHAPTER 38

MIA

A nurse grabbed my hand. "Please, Mia, let's get you to the waiting room."

I stood up onto two trembling legs and stumbled to the waiting room. Tears raced down my cheeks—I could barely see through the tears in my eyes—and loud, shuddering sobs were escaping my throat.

And when I turned the corner into the waiting room, I found the first open seat and collapsed down into it, curling up into a ball and crying my eyes out. Every time someone came over to me, I pushed them away. I wanted to sit alone. I *needed* to sit alone. I had dealt with this before by myself that it felt too weird to have all these people here with me.

I waited for what seemed like days, but it was only hours, nestled in the hospital chair with my knees to my chest and tears streaming down my face. Mom had sounded so defeated, like she didn't even want to live anymore. And honestly, I didn't blame her. Life had dealt her a shitty hand—from Dad to *two* aneurysms. If I were her, I'd think the same way.

Sometime during the day, Michael walked over to me and crouched by my side, asking me if I was okay or if I wanted something to eat. But I couldn't even look him in the eye. Melissa sat across from me, swinging her legs back and forth and staring aimlessly at the ground. I didn't even know why she was here. It was clear from the last time I had seen her that she didn't want anything to do with me.

The door to the waiting room opened, and my heart skipped a beat. I didn't want to know if I *wanted* to know the outcome of Mom's surgery yet. But I stood up anyway and tried my hardest to push back the tears. But instead of seeing a doctor, a man hobbled into the room with a walker. He pushed the silver bars across the white tiled floor and smiled at me.

"Mia," he said, his voice shaky and gruff. "Has your mother gone into surgery yet?"

I furrowed my brows at him, and then my eyes widened. "James?"

I hadn't seen James in four years—since the last time Mom had been in the ICU. He had been recovering from a stroke. Mom had grown quite fond of him when she was here, as their rooms were across from each other's. Every time I came to visit, he always made her laugh. But when they moved her out, she lost contact with him. Or at least, I'd thought she did.

He gave me a weak smile and nodded, sitting down in the seat beside me. "Long time since I've seen you, kiddo." James clasped his hands in his lap, eyes growing wide.

"What are you doing here?" I asked, brows furrowed.

"I'm here to see your mother. We've been sending letters back and forth ever since she left." He reached behind him and into his back pocket, pulling out a bunch of envelopes. "These bad boys."

He handed them over to me, and I opened one up, my lips pulling into a smile.

In it, there were a handful of letters on ripped napkins or coffee-stained paper from the assisted living home. Mom's handwriting decorated all of them, and she left cute little smiley faces at the bottom. She even signed one with *Love, Eden.*

My heart swelled, and I clasped it to my chest. Mom had to survive. She had to. I'd thought her life had been so shitty, but she'd found happiness in even the smallest things.

I handed the envelopes back to James and grasped his shoulder. "Mom is still in surgery, but ... I don't know if she'll make it."

He gave a gruff laugh. "She'd better. I plan to take her on my vacation with me soon, maybe in the fall. I've been saving up enough money to bring her out." He looked up at me. "I've been getting better."

I squeezed his shoulder a little tighter. "She'd love that," I whispered.

Though James was almost twenty years older than Mom—nearing sixty-five—I could tell that he'd make her smile. But ... I wondered why Mom hadn't told me about him. Was it the age gap? Had she been afraid to tell me she had been talking to someone after Dad? Maybe she hadn't said anything because she didn't know if it was serious between them yet or if they'd ever really be able to be together.

Whatever the reason, I was beyond glad that he was here for her. She'd told me that I needed to be strong, that I needed the right kind of love. Well, so did she. And she deserved it more than anyone. Mom had better make it. She had her entire life ahead of her. No matter her age, no matter how shitty her life had been so far, she was a fighter, and she'd fight this.

James held out his hand, and I placed mine in it, squeezing. I stared at Michael, my heart feeling lighter than it had before. I hoped, prayed, waited for a long time before Michael came over again, crouching next to me.

He took my free hand and smiled. "It's going to be okay, Mia. No matter what happens with your mother, I've got you."

My heart warmed, and I smiled down at him. Though I was sitting in the hospital as Mom was in surgery, something felt ... better. In some fucked up way, I felt like I was finally in a good place. I had people who were here to support me. I had friends and—I glanced down at Michael—family who would be there when I needed them.

"I know," I said, and for the first time in a long time, I meant it.

He nodded to the seat next to me. "Can I sit?"

I patted the seat beside me and curled my arm around his, resting my head on his shoulder. Melissa gazed at us from across the room, and I didn't know if she was glaring or just staring. I wasn't sure I wanted to know. At some point, we'd have to work things out, but I didn't want the drama right now.

I intertwined my fingers with his, my eyes closing gently. After what seemed like days of waiting, Dr. Jackson walked into the waiting room.

"Mia," he said, lips pressed into a tight line.

I shot up from my seat almost instantly, my stomach dropping. "What's wrong? Is everything okay? When can I see her?" I asked, hoping to God that she'd made it.

James stood up next to me and placed a shaky hand on my shoulder, nodding to the doctor who had done surgery on him too.

Dr. Jackson paused for a moment and glanced around. "Your mother had some complications during her surgery..."

My heart stopped.

"But she is in recovery as we speak."

I stood there in complete disbelief. After the complications bit, all I'd expected to hear was that she'd passed away.

I shook my head. "What did you say?" I asked, my voice small.

"Your mother is recovering, but—"

But? I didn't care about the "but" right now. All I cared about was getting to see Mom again—alive. By the way she had talked earlier, I'd thought I would lose her for good. I'd thought I'd never see her again.

I threw my arms around him, not even able to cry happy tears. But I was beyond happy. I was ecstatic, gleeful, and so fucking thrilled. "Thank you. Thank you. Thank you. Thank you."

"Mia, please, let me speak," Dr. Jackson said after a few moments, gently pushing me away.

Michael grabbed my shoulders and pulled me off of him. "Let him tell you about the complications before you get excited," he whispered in my ear.

My smile dropped, and I nodded to let him speak.

"A couple days ago, we found a blood clot in your mother's brain, which can happen after brain surgery for aneurysms, especially after two. So, today we inserted a catheter to help the blood flow, but in recovery, we noticed your mother acting ... *different*."

I held my breath, my palms sweating, and listened to him. "Different how?"

"In her right eye, there's some peripheral damage," he said. "Her speech is a bit slurred at the moment. And she is having minor memory problems."

"She won't remember me?" I asked quietly, my heart sinking in my chest. "My mom won't remember me?"

"I believe she will. We've run a couple tests, and we think she's having some trouble with forming new memories. This usually lasts between a few minutes to months, but I can't tell you for sure when she'll recover from this."

My heart sank, but I tried to keep a strong mind. Mom was alive. That was what I had hoped for, and maybe not remembering this time in the hospital might be good for her ... but I had a feeling it wouldn't be.

CHAPTER 39

MIA

"Mom," I said, throwing my arms around her shoulders and pulling her into a tight hug as soon as I could. The doctor had said she might not be able to make new memories anytime soon, but that didn't mean I couldn't. "You made it."

She wrapped her arms around me and laughed into my chest. "I did, sweetheart. All those tears were for nothing," she said, but there wasn't reassurance in her words.

I didn't want to tell her I had lost faith in her recovery or her ability to withstand another surgery, so I smacked my lips closed and enjoyed our moment together.

This was what I'd do from now on. No more Mason telling me when I could and couldn't see her. No more Mason holding me back from spending all the damn time I could with Mom. She was mine, and I wasn't going to let her go.

"Melissa is here," Mom said, nodding over to the window. Her eyes landed on James, who stood outside, tilting his hat toward her. She broke out into a big smile, then turned back to me. "You should go talk to her."

Though I really didn't want to talk to her right now, I kissed Mom's forehead and walked out of the room, holding the door open for James. Almost immediately, I could hear Mom's laugh, and everything felt so much better. She might not remember today or tomorrow or the next few months—which would hurt—but at least she was happy.

My gaze met Melissa's, and I nodded toward a more private area of the waiting room because there were far too many people here. I didn't know what I was going to say to her, but I wanted to let her know that this wasn't how it was supposed to be and that she shouldn't date Mason. Mom wanted me to make things right with her, and I would at least try.

When I reached the waiting room, I sat in an empty corner, wanting our conversation to be private. Well, as private as it could. I could see Michael watching us intently from across the room. His daughter and I were fighting. He couldn't choose one or the other, and I wouldn't let him choose. I wanted Melissa to have a good relationship with her father because I never could have one, and her mother seemed like a big asshole.

"Hey," Melissa said, sitting next to me.

I gulped and glanced over at her. "Hey."

In my heart, I knew that we needed to talk. And now that Mom's surgery was over, I could breathe for a few moments. But … I didn't know what to say to her. That I was fucking her dad and that I loved him? That Mason was a total asshole?

But I had to say something, so I turned to her at the same time she turned to me.

"I need to—"

"Don't see Mas—"

We both paused at the same time, and then she urged me to go on. I took a deep breath. I didn't know how serious she was about Mason, but I needed to warn her before something bad happened to her. Michael had cut her off for a good reason—to teach her responsibility and respect—but she was susceptible to the same abuse that I had been.

"Don't see Mason unless you're serious about him. I didn't tell you how bad he abused me because ... because I didn't see it at the time. Don't let him control you. Don't let things go when you know something is up. He's ... not a good guy. He'll gaslight you. He'll get jealous. He'll try to hurt you with words. If you need anything, ask Mich—your father."

"He cut me off," she said, her words coming out harsh.

I knew that I was the reason he'd cut her off, but I wanted her to grow up too. She couldn't party for the rest of her life at frats with men who didn't give a fuck about her.

"Your father will still help you if you change and realize your mistakes."

Her lips twisted into a menacing scowl. "Don't try to be my mom, Mia. You're my friend," she said with so much disdain.

I parted my lips to argue with her, then pressed them back together. Both of those titles seemed off right now. I wasn't her mom, and I wasn't trying to be her mom, but I also wasn't her friend. I didn't know if our friendship could recover from this.

"I'm not trying to be your mother. I just want you to know that he loves you, no matter what," I said. "You should appreciate what he's done for you because not any father or mother could or would do that."

"He kicked me out," she said again through gritted teeth.

"Well, you need to grow up, Melissa," I said, getting angry. "You can't live off of his money for the rest of your life." The words felt wrong, coming from me, because I had used Mason for his money for years, but I had also worked while staying with him. I chipped in when I could. I paid for Mom's piling hospital bills. I had done it all even though I should've been focusing on school. But Mom deserved it. "It'll be good for you, and you'll add experience to your résumé when you apply to jobs in the future."

She stayed quiet for a long time with her arms crossed over her chest and her focus fixed on the floor. "How long have you been fucking my dad?" she asked. The question came out quietly and with so much spite, yet I knew Michael heard it from across the room.

"It happened a month ago, maybe a bit longer." I frowned. Everything had been going on lately that I couldn't keep track of my months anymore. "I never meant for this thing between me and him to be anything more than physical," I said, staring her right in the eye. I'd promised Mom that I wouldn't take any shit from anyone anymore, and I didn't plan on letting myself feel bad over my feelings toward Michael because they were so fucking beautiful and not anything I had ever experienced before. "It started as something to help blow off steam."

Melissa's nose scrunched up, and she looked away, staying quiet for more than a few seconds. Then, she blew a deep breath from her nose. "I can't believe you're fucking my fucking father."

"I can't believe that you fucked my boyfriend, and still are sleeping with that asshole," I said, tired of this argument only being one-sided.

I took the blame, yes, but she wasn't innocent either, and she needed to understand that what she had done was wrong too.

"It's not the same."

"No, it's not." I crossed my arms over my chest. "But it still happened."

She shook her head. So many emotions crossed her face—betrayal, hurt, and shame. Yet I didn't know what to say to her to make it better—nor did I know if I wanted to make this better or to try to salvage our relationship. After another moment, she stood and walked over to the elevator, disappearing into it.

I sighed through my nose and glanced up at Serena, who stood in front of me.

She sat in the seat Melissa had. "Do you think you'll ever be friends again?"

My heart hurt. I wouldn't be able to trust her for a long time, and honestly, I didn't know if she'd be able to trust me. We'd both fucked up big time. And I didn't want to be hurt again. I shrugged and glanced at Michael, who was talking to James now.

For his sake, I'd try my hardest to be friends with her eventually, but I couldn't promise that anything would come of it. Our friendship hadn't ever been broken this badly before.

CHAPTER 40

MIA

It had been two long and tortuous weeks since Mom's surgery. Since my chat with Melissa, I had barely seen her. She seemed to be ignoring me, as she had come over to see Michael once in the morning, when I was at the hospital, but that was it. As far as I knew, she was living it up with Mason in his luxury apartment, acting like things were perfect, acting like the perfect girlfriend, like I had at one point.

But I would continue to ask Michael about her every now and then. I didn't want her to end up like I had. When I saw the signs, I'd make sure she knew them, too, no matter how much she didn't want me to butt into her *amazing* relationship. I would because I cared about her even though I shouldn't.

I sat across from Michael at a restaurant, feeling like a fraud. I hadn't been out to dinner in weeks, and sitting here in a pretty black dress with my makeup done and my hair curled made me feel … weird, to say the least. Michael liked it—that much I could tell.

He sat across from me in a black suit, his hair wet and parted to the side, gray eyes on me. Just by the way he looked at me and only me, the way he gave me his full attention, instead of ogling some other girls, it made me feel good on the inside. It was a feeling I hoped never went away.

"Hi, I'm Alicia, and I'll be taking care of you tonight," a young woman said, smiling between us.

She went over some specials—half of what she said I couldn't even pronounce, but I didn't mind.

I gave her my order and sipped on my white wine. There was so much I wanted to talk about tonight, but I didn't even know where to start. I decided to keep my mouth shut though. Tonight was supposed to be a happy, feel-good kind of night, and I didn't want to ruin it with my problems.

Michael would say that it wasn't ruining it, but for me, it would. This night was about us.

So, we had dinner and dessert, finished an entire bottle of wine, and talked all night long. About anything and everything, and I learned things that I hadn't even known about him before. It was cliché, but it was so real and so raw for once.

I scraped some frosting off my plate with my fork and stuffed it into my mouth. Michael talked about his work, smiling at me with so much pride that it made my heart warm. A candle flickered between us, illuminating his perfect face.

Before I could stop myself, I leaned over the table and placed a kiss right on his mouth. This man … God, I loved this man with all my heart, and this feeling wasn't going away. He had been there for me since Mom had had her second aneurysm, had stayed with me night after night, had given me a place to stay and security without making me feel bad about it. He was everything I could ever ask for in a man and so much more.

He kissed me back, his fingers brushing against mine on the table.

When I pulled away, I gathered all the courage I had inside of me. "I love you, Michael."

Michael sat, wide-eyed, across from me, a million emotions crossing his face. My heart skipped a beat, and I wanted to take it all back. It was probably too much.

"Sorry if it's too soon," I said, rubbing my palms on my dress. "I know how I feel and—"

Before I could speak another word, he cupped my face and pressed his lips back to mine in a heated, open-mouthed kiss. "Oh, Mia," he said against me. "I love you so much more. I've been waiting for you to say it. I didn't know if it was the right time."

Butterflies fluttered in my stomach, and I smiled so widely.

Michael loved me too.

He pulled out his wallet, grabbed a few bills, and threw them onto the table. Then, he took my hand and pulled me to the back of the restaurant.

"God, I can't wait to have you." Without even checking, he pushed open the restroom door, his lips all over my neck from behind. His hands were roaming my body, touching every part of me that he could.

He kicked the door closed with his foot and locked it. My heart was pounding against my chest at the thought of being caught, but I didn't want to stop now. I wanted him here.

The restroom was cleaner than any other public restroom I had been in with granite countertops, porcelain sinks, and a large mirror with dimmed accent lights. He pushed me against the counter and plunged his fingers under my dress and into my panties. I stared into the mirror, watching his dark eyes devour every inch of my body. In and out and in and out, his fingers moved so fucking fast that I had to clutch on to the sink for support.

His palm hit against my clit, and I closed my eyes, letting the heat build. I moved my hips ever so slowly against his fingers, riding them. He sucked on the skin just below my ear and groaned against me.

"You're so wet, baby." He slammed his fingers up into me, thumb rubbing against my clit.

I moved my hips back and forth, the tension rising in my core. The friction against my clit was driving me crazy. I needed this man, and I needed him now.

"Please, Michael," I whimpered.

He curled his hand around my neck and pulled me to him, undoing my dress zipper.

Without him asking, I pulled the top of my dress off my shoulders and unclipped my bra, letting my breasts fall out of it. I couldn't wait any longer to have his hands on them. He groped one of my breasts in his hand and rolled my nipple against his palm, making me tighten.

I bit my lip and moaned. He tugged on my nipple, his fingers slamming up into me, and heat warmed my pussy. The tension was enough to send me right over the edge until I doubled over on the countertop, my fingers digging into the smooth granite.

My body seized back and forth, the ecstasy rushing out of me. He turned on the sink, splashed some water on my tits to make them wet and glistening, and pressed his hardness against me from behind.

"Fuck, Mia." He pulled his fingers out of my pussy and stuck them into my mouth, watching me intently. "You drive me wild."

My body shuddered against him, my mind foggy with ecstasy. He picked me up and placed me on the countertop, stood between my legs, and pulled off my panties, stuffing them into my mouth. He pulled me to the edge and crouched between my legs. He massaged my clit with his tongue, moving it in small, torturous circles.

I laced my fingers in his hair, pulling him closer to me, and moaned as loudly as I could with my panties stuffed into my mouth. His tongue was doing wonders, his fingers playing with my entrance again. He took my chin and made me watch him please me. I clenched around his fingers, my legs shaking. But this time, he didn't let me come again.

Instead, he spit on my clit and rubbed it all over my pussy, getting it wet and ready for him. After pulling me off the counter, he turned me around and forced me to spread my legs from behind. He pulled my panties out of my mouth and threw them onto the counter next to us, and then he took his cock in his hand, rubbed it against my wetness, and made it glisten with my juices.

He grabbed a fistful of my hair and slammed hard into me from behind. I let out a loud moan, and he pulled my body against his, starting to pound into me and watching my tits move in the mirror. I stared at him, my pussy pulsing.

"Michael," I whispered.

He wrapped his arms around my torso, groping my tits, and then sucked on my neck. I curled my toes, another moan escaping my lips. A wave of pleasure rolled through me.

"Please, Michael. More."

He continued to suck me as he pumped in and out of me faster until I could barely hold myself up. I threw my head back, giving him better access, and he tugged on my nipples.

"Keep tightening your pussy on me," he said into my ear.

I clenched on him, the force building in my pussy. He groaned and let go of my nipples, letting my breasts bounce in his hands. The rapture shot through me, and I arched my back, another orgasm cutting through me. He continued to thrust into me until I felt his warm cum pumping out of my hole.

And when he finally pulled out of me, he pressed his lips on my bare shoulder. "I love you so fucking much, Mia."

CHAPTER 41

MIA

Michael planted a kiss on my lips and rolled off of me, staring up at the ceiling. "Mia, you're going to kill me with all this sex," he said, chuckling and breathing heavy. The sunlight flooded in through the sheer curtains and shone against his sweaty chest, rising and falling with every breath.

I rolled onto my stomach, kicking my legs back and forth, and smiled at him. He glanced down at me, lips pulled into a smile too. It had been a couple days since I'd told Michael I loved him, and we'd been having sex whenever we could. This honeymoon phase would wear off soon, but I couldn't keep my hands off of him now.

On the other hand, Mom was recovering quicker than the doctors had expected. I thought it was because James sat by her bed all day, every day, cracking jokes and telling her that she'd better get healthier soon, that they had so much to do in their lives together.

Mom was happy. I rested my fingers on Michael's chest. And so was I.

"You're not saying you want to stop having sex, are you?" I asked playfully, brow raised.

He chuckled and pulled me onto his chest. "No."

His eyes were ocean blue, and I wanted to stare into them forever. They were so damn beautiful, and they were all mine.

"I would never want to stop loving you."

My heart fluttered. Usually, by now, the butterflies would've worn off—at least, they had with Mason—but I still felt them, and that made me feel so fucking good on the inside.

"Breakfast in half an hour?" he asked. "We could go to your favorite place?"

"And get pancakes with strawberries?" I asked, curling my fingers into his chest.

"Anything you want."

I stared at him in awe and nodded. Things weren't perfect. They were far from it, but this was what I wanted. For the first time in my entire life, I got to choose who I was with and who I could be happy with. And I finally had a man who was mine.

"I'm going to shower first," Michael said, kissing me. "Care to join me?"

I pushed him toward our bathroom. "Maybe later," I said.

There was so much schoolwork that had piled up these past few weeks that I had to do. I was taking summer classes to catch up on my missed first semester.

"I have to do some work for school."

"There's always room." He winked and walked back into the bathroom, his back muscles flexing.

If I didn't have self-restraint, I'd hop right into the shower with him and let him take me the rest of the day.

But I had shit to do—shit that would help me get a better future. So, I plopped down at the kitchen table and opened my laptop. All of my missed work from the past week popped up along with emails from some of my professors, asking me how my mother was doing.

I started on my psych homework, reading through the textbook and trying to concentrate. My phone buzzed on the table, and I glanced at it, seeing Mason's number pop up on the screen. I opened the phone, reading the message. He hadn't texted me in a couple of weeks. Why was he sudden—

Mason: Can I see you?

Almost a second later, another message appeared.

Mason: Please, I want to talk.

I rolled my eyes and shut the phone off, so it wouldn't be a distraction. I didn't want to delete the conversation or his number, so if I needed to, I could provide Melissa with proof that he wouldn't ever appreciate her. I doubted she'd actually believe me, but it was worth a shot.

After silencing my phone, I continued reading about different abnormalities in the brain, trying to understand what was happening to Mom and her memory. But someone obviously didn't want me to study today because they knocked on the front door.

I raised my brow and glanced at the door, eyeing it to see if it was Mason. He would be the one to show up and ruin my entire life. When I caught a glimpse of Melissa's blonde hair through one of the door windows, I hopped up from my seat and walked down the stairs.

I didn't really like answering other people's doors, but Michael was in the shower, washing off from that amazing sex. When I opened the door though, it wasn't Melissa.

I sucked in a deep breath, my eyes widening at the woman standing before me. I hadn't seen her in years, but she hadn't changed one bit. Melissa's mother stood at the front door, a Gucci purse hanging off her forearm and a fake smile plastered on her face.

"Hi, Mia. Is Michael home?"

Continue to Book 2 here!

ALSO BY EMILIA ROSE

Paranormal Romance

Submitting to the Alpha: https://books2read.com/u/4N9Bd6

Come Here, Kitten: https://books2read.com/u/b55dol

Alpha Maddox: https://books2read.com/u/bPXP8l

My Werewolf Professor: https://books2read.com/my-werewolf-professor

The Twins: https://books2read.com/the-twins

Four Masked Wolves: https://www.patreon.com/emiliarosewriting

Contemporary Romance

Poison: https://books2read.com/Poison-Redwood-Academy

Stepbrother: https://books2read.com/Stepbrother-Redwood-Academy

Excite Me: https://books2read.com/excite-me

Erotica

Climax: https://books2read.com/u/4XrBka

ABOUT THE AUTHOR

Emilia Rose is an international best-selling author of steamy romance. Highly inspired by her study abroad trip to Greece in 2019, Emilia loves to include Greek and Roman mythology in her writing.

She graduated from the University of Pittsburgh with a degree in psychology and a minor in creative writing in 2020 and now writes novels as her day job.

With over 18 million combined book views online and a growing presence on reading apps, she hopes to inspire other young novelists with her tales of growth and imagination, so they go on to write the stories that need to be told.

Join Emilia's newsletter for exclusive news > https://www.emiliarosewriting.com/

Manufactured by Amazon.ca
Acheson, AB